"Bourke does an exceller
and hardworking young woman who is quick to admit and relinquish
her prejudices and cares deeply about the animals in her care even
when she is supposed to affect professional detachment. The novel is
engagingly written and never drags or dithers … An affecting portrayal
of the making of a veterinarian and the day-to-day challenges she faces."

— *Kirkus'* Indie Books of the Month Selection

"Rita Welty Bourke weaves an intricate web of stories that showcase
her marvelous talents as a writer. Her sensitive, insightful portrayal
of animals in the wild and in domestic settings is one of the great joys
in store for the reader. Rich and lyrical in their delivery, the stories in
Kylie's Ark are a powerful, profound examination of the heart and soul
of a young veterinarian and the forces that shape the world she has
chosen for her profession."

—Phyllis Gobbell, author of *A Season of Darkness*
and *Pursuit in Provence*

"For those who have ever pondered the life of a veterinary student or
a young veterinary professional, *Kylie's Ark* is the read for you. It is a
heartwarming and raw look at the trials and tribulations one experiences
in vet school and in the professional world of veterinary medicine. The
book highlights the compassion and humor that are required when
one dedicates one's life to reducing the suffering of animals. *Kylie's Ark*
is a treasure."

—Jennifer Saunders, DVM, Willamette Valley Equine
Veterinary Services, Portland, Oregon

KYLIE'S
ARK

KYLIE'S ARK

*The Making of a
Veterinarian*

RITA WELTY BOURKE

Published in the United States by Lansinger Press.

Library of Congress Control Number: 2015941911

ISBN 978-0-9964201-0-5

Some of the stories in this work were previously published in a slightly different form in the following: "Gunnison Beach" in *Witness* and in the anthology *Naked*, "The Extern" in *The Florida Review*, "From Farrow to Fork" in the *North American Review*, and "Dominion" in the *Cimarron Review*.

Book design by BourkeDesign.com

Author photograph by Rory Bourke

for my daughters

"Know that the same spark of life that is within you,
is within all of our animal friends,
the desire to live is the same within all of us ..."

—Rai Aren, *Secret of the Sands*

Contents

PROLOGUE

KYLIE WHEELER was in her last year of veterinary school when one of her rotations took her into the Texas prison system. She and three of her classmates, working under the supervision of a Texas A&M professor, de-wormed horses, inserted nasogastric tubes, bled pigs, collected fecal material, and spayed bloodhounds. It was a chance to acquire massive amounts of experience working with non-client-owned animals. Should they make a mistake, the guards were unlikely to notice, or to care.

For the duration of the two-week rotation the vet students arrived at their assigned prison by 6 a.m., worked until noon, ate a prison-provided lunch, then resumed their tasks until 4 p.m.

Prisons in Texas are largely self-sustaining; they grow much of their food and raise cattle and pigs. They keep horses for the use of prison guards and bloodhounds to chase down escapees.

The female students were advised to wear one-piece green overall scrubs. No make-up or perfume.

Kylie's job at the first prison farm was to palpate a dozen cattle to determine if they were pregnant. Among the supplies Kylie brought with her that day was a box of arm-length disposable gloves.

Prisoners drove the cattle into the enclosure, Kylie did the examinations, and the prisoners released the animals while Kylie recorded the results. One inmate seemed especially troubled by the procedure. He hovered near where Kylie was working, but he did not speak.

Kylie felt something brush against her. She looked, and saw that the prisoner was tugging at her glove, pulling it up so that it extended onto her shoulder. Not knowing how to respond, wondering if she should even notice, Kylie continued the examination. He was being careful not to actually touch her, she realized. But he was clearly worried the glove would slip, and she would be soiled.

Later, she learned that the prisoner, like most of the inmates assigned to this work detail, was a lifer. He'd killed three men during a bank robbery.

This vignette did not find its way into the stories that follow, but it happened. As did all the tales in this book.

Andy, Kylie's boyfriend at the time and now her husband, never likes to hear Kylie tell the story. He thinks the prisoner was making a pass. Kylie denies this. She insists the inmate was being chivalrous.

The stories are Kylie's stories. I wrote them down much as she gave them to me. In certain cases I've altered names, changed locations and sequences. Some she gave to me so complete, so full of her, all I needed to do was write until my hand hurt and my fingers grew numb. Some I had to flesh out, because I knew things about her the reader needed to know in order to understand who she is and what kind of person she became. Some I had to let simmer while she tried to work things out in her mind.

The path she chose to follow presented dilemmas that challenged her in ways she could not have imagined. As the idealism of youth is tempered by the realities of life, so too Kylie was tested, tempered, and forged, but she never gave up the struggle to hold onto the things she most cherished.

I am not Kylie, though I know her well. I use her voice, I speak through her, and I have tried to be faithful to her.

GUNNISON BEACH

THEY CALL US PARK SERVICE BITCHES: Geneva Hartland, Sallie Bailey, and me, Kylie Wheeler from Birmingham, Alabama. This past May I walked off the stage at the University of Colorado with a ribbon around my neck, a medallion hanging between my breasts, and a leather-bound diploma swinging from my fingertips. That's how I snagged this job with the National Park Service. The federal government is impressed with stuff like that.

We walk, and sometimes ride, the beaches at Sandy Hook, New Jersey, wearing Department of Interior outfits: olive green shorts and matching blouses with insignias on the shoulders, Vasque boots, and wide-brim hats. We put on sunglasses, sunblock, and insect repellent before we venture out of our housing units. Sallie and I live in old army barracks that date from pre-Civil War days.

A biological science technician, GS 5 level, I was hired to protect endangered species on the island. Specifically, I am to document sightings of black skimmers, least terns, and piping plovers. I am to follow them through their mating and nesting cycles and protect them from harm.

I carry government-issue, high-powered binoculars. Sometimes, in the pursuit of my duties, I have to become a Park Service Police Officer. Hence the name: Park Service Bitch.

Sallie is an intern, unpaid except for free housing and uniforms. She dreams of getting a job with Greenpeace one day.

Geneva is our boss.

The swimmers and sunbathers who come over from the mainland don't like it when we close their beaches, which we do from time to time. And the nudies up on Gunnison don't like women who are clothed coming into their private world. Mostly gay and largely male, they especially dislike women in positions of authority.

Right off the bat, one of them got smart with me about roping off an area of the beach where he wanted to set up a badminton court.

"Every year you're taking more of the beach away from us," he whined. "I'm a taxpayer, like everyone else. I have rights."

Yeah, right. Get a life, Mister. "Sir, we're here to protect the piping plovers. We have no control over where they decide to nest. Our job is to find the nests, build an exclosure, and rope off the surrounding area. If you have a problem with that, write your congressman. He voted for the Endangered Species Act." Get out of my way. I have a job to do.

Geneva trained us to be tough. Uncompromising. Anyone who won't listen, throw them off the island, she said. Ban them from coming onto the Hook for the rest of the season. And don't hesitate to call security if you need extra muscle.

She handed me a radio, which I hooked onto my belt. It became part of my uniform.

Geneva takes nothin' off nobody. She's been here seven years, and she's seen it all.

She just got tossed out of her house because she let her boyfriend move in with her. The government frowns on what they call "fraternization." Since her eviction, Geneva's been in a constant state of mad.

Yet she can be soft in ways that catch you unexpectedly. Like last week, when she went after some New York City trash who decided to picnic inside one of our nesting areas. She grabbed one of our signs off the truck and waved it in their faces. "Can't you read English? Do you understand what this says? A-R-E-A C-L-O-S-E-D?" She was so mad she sprayed spit when she spelled out the letters.

It was a family of foreign-looking people who probably did not speak English. They never said a word, just looked scared and backed away from her. The father ushered his wife and carbon-copy kids under the wire, and they scrambled off as fast as hermit crabs.

The nest had been trampled. The two plovers scampered around on the sand, one of them doing the broken wing act, trying to draw us away from the nest.

"She thinks her babies are still alive," Geneva said. She walked over to the smoothed-out hollow in the sand.

All four eggs were squashed, the nest wet with mucous. You could see the imprint of a kid's shoe; he'd run right through it.

Geneva hunkered down and picked up a piece of broken egg, and I thought she would cry. She held it in the palm of her hand, just looking at it for the longest time. "It was no more than a day or two from hatching," she said.

With Sallie and me looking on, it felt as if we were attending a funeral there on the beach.

Inside the curve of the shell was a wet cotton ball. Geneva touched its beak, its orange legs, its tiny feet.

Baby plovers look like puffs of cotton stuck on orange toothpicks. This one would never run on the beach, never do the broken wing trick, never have a nest of its own.

Damn stupid people.

I arrived on the island during a thunderstorm that cut the electricity, doubled trees over, and nearly toppled the lighthouse up on the north shore. I spent the night huddled in an empty dorm room wondering why I ever left Boulder, wishing I'd brought a flashlight, praying the ocean didn't rear up and sweep right over the island.

The next morning I had to clean up the road that runs down the spine of the island. In the afternoon I set fox traps. And I saw my first nude, an old gay man jogging on the road well beyond the area where he should have been.

I let him go. He was wearing a shirt, so he wasn't totally nude. And with my new uniform still stiff from the sizing, I could afford to wait another day or two.

That first week I caught a feral cat, but I let her go, too. She was a nursing mother, and she'd eaten every bit of the raw chicken I'd tied to the tripwire inside the cage. Her belly was puffed out with chicken and her breasts swollen with milk.

Geneva was ready to send me packing for that. "Don't you realize she'll eat the birds as soon as they hatch?" Sand birds who run on the beach, preferring to walk rather than fly, are no match for a hungry mother cat with kittens hidden away. "Find her kittens and take them over to the shelter in Red Bank," she ordered.

But I never did. The mother cat avoided the trap after that. She was as smart as the foxes, who are doomed. I've seen the paperwork on Geneva's desk; the Park Service plans to gas the dens in the spring.

I did catch one fox and managed to find him a home. The Bronx Zoo agreed to ship him down to the Great Smoky Mountains, where he can live with others of his species. If he's lucky, he might be able to catch one of the wild pigs that threaten the delicate balance park officials strive to maintain.

When I learned the fate of other foxes that might wander into my traps, I made some changes. I quit scrubbing off the traces of fox blood. I neglected to remove my own scent from the cages. I even sprayed some of the trap doors with perfume I borrowed from Sallie's makeup bag. All this kept his brothers at a distance, safe from the ranger's pistol.

The zoo officials put my fox in a cage lined with the *New York Post*. They joked that he could read about Bill Clinton's sex life on his plane ride to Tennessee. And if that didn't interest him, he could look at the picture of the newborn baby found in a dumpster in Queens.

Sometimes we ride the Park Service horses around the island, and sometimes we take the Jeep. We use the Jeep when we have to carry fencing to build exclosures and barriers around the plover nests. We have 42 nesting pairs here on the island, which is about a third of all the piping plovers left in the world.

Geneva says last year the park service was able to document 72 hatchling chicks. So far this summer only four babies have fledged.

Occasionally we find fox tracks around the empty nests. The cats and sea gulls take a toll, as do summer storms and high tides. But it's the people who are the worst offenders. They drive across the bridge and crowd in here, walk over the nests, flop down on the beach with never a thought as to what they might be destroying.

Weekends we Bitches are out in force, hiding behind the dunes, guarding the nesting areas. It's getting so I like my nickname, because it means I'm doing my job.

I'm busy sledge hammering posts into the sand up on Kingman Beach when the old nude man approaches me.

"I've been watching you building these pens for days, sweetie. Why are you doing it?" He puts an arm around me, jostles me as if I were a child.

"The nests are hard to see, sir," I tell him, twisting away from him. "But they're here." I wipe an arm across my nose; he smells of coconut oil and something else I can't identify.

"I haven't seen a birdie all day, darlin'," he says. The shirt from that first day is gone. He wears three earrings. Nothing else. "Maybe they've gone somewhere else."

"They're shore birds," I tell him. "They have nowhere else to go. This is where they live. Once there were millions. All up and down the coast. Now there are a few hundred."

"Maybe I could help you," he says, and moves to take the hammer from me.

But I tell him to get himself back to Gunnison where he belongs. I drum my fingers on the steel post and watch to make sure he goes in the right direction.

Some of the nudies like to be looked at. When they see our Jeep approaching, they strut their stuff. As if we care about their appendages and piercings and wacko jewelry. Sallie, raised a Baptist, looks the other way. Nude is bad enough, she says. Nude and gay is over the top.

Geneva says they think we spy on them, hide behind the dunes with our binoculars, hoping to gather evidence so we can close their beach. But who cares what they do down there? As long as they leave the birds alone.

"Chill out, lady," the fisherman says, kicking sand in my direction. "I'm not anywhere near your birds."

"You're in a restricted area," I tell him. "You'll have to leave."

"The nests are way up there on the hill," he argues. He takes a crab off his line and throws it to the waiting sea gulls. They scramble to grab their prize. The winners tear it to pieces.

"The plovers have to come down to the intertidal area to feed," I tell him. "When the tide goes out, that's the richest feeding ground. That's why we rope it off down to the water. You'll have to go somewhere else."

He throws another crab to a gull who stands apart from the others. The bird gobbles it down, his beak twisting like a knife in the hands of a Jersey City gangster.

I notice that the gull has only one leg, and I wonder who to feel sorry for, bird or crab.

"Why don't you go get laid," the fisherman says, winding in his line, gathering up his equipment.

I stand very still, wondering what Geneva would do.

"You can't walk through this exclosure, sir," I tell him. I plant my legs wide and solid in the sand and jerk my radio off my belt.

"Just how am I supposed to get around your precious bird sanctuary?"

"Walk up to the road, sir. Walk along the road until you find a path down to an area that is not roped off." I tap a fingernail against the plastic on my radio.

He picks up his gear and moves off.

One month on the job and I'm frustrated and angry. Geneva tells me to take a break. "Saddle up one of the horses and go for a ride," she says. "Hurricane needs a good workout. Take him over to Hidden Cove and look for fox dens and terns. Have a picnic on the beach."

I saddle the chestnut gelding, and we race along the water's edge for most of the morning. We swim across to Skeleton Island, and I marvel at the blue herons and snowy egrets and oystercatchers.

There have never been piping plovers at Hidden Cove, but this year they're all over the beach. Hurricane and I round an outcropping of rock, and I spot half a dozen nesting pairs. Babies and adult birds rush about helter-skelter, more birds than I can count.

I sit on my horse thinking this is the way it used to be. Geneva is miles away, but I want to call out to her to come look. I want to slap my horse on the rump and fly up to the lighthouse and send her a signal, *come quick, Geneva, come see what I found.*

The tide is out and the birds are active. They scamper down to the water's edge, grab an insect or some interesting piece of flotsam, run back to the nest, or just zigzag around in bursts of energy. There are no predators, and the plovers are thriving.

I tether Hurricane to a piece of driftwood and settle down in the sand to document what I'm seeing. I make notes in my field book, map out the nests, estimate the number and ages of the babies. As the day advances, the heat, the lapping water, and the lovely sight of the peeping sand birds work their magic on me. Nestled in the warm sand, I doze off.

I'm awakened by rap music booming from a portable radio, its insistent rhythm sending an electric shock through the air. The plovers have never heard such noise; they take cover wherever they can.

A group of boys comes dancing up the beach. They wear oversized jeans that drag in the sand. I move behind a ridge of rocks.

One of the boys kicks an empty Coke can into a tuft of sea grass, and three plovers run out, chirping fearfully. They're sand colored and orange with black stripes between their eyes and around their necks. They run about in melee, their hiding place discovered, the music reverberating between the water and the rock-strewn dunes.

"Let's get 'em," one of the boys yells, and they swing into action. They herd the plovers away from the protective dunes, toward the sea. One plover is cut off from his nest mates, and he cries out. His pursuer falls on top of him. When the boy rises, he looks down at the captured bird. It does not move.

I toss my notebook aside and come roaring out of my hiding place, yelling, racing down the incline. But the surf pounds and the boom box blares, and the boys pay me no mind.

They pick up pieces of driftwood and begin to beat the mounds of grass, looking for more birds, shooing the babies out from their shelters. They chase after them, driving them into the sea, up onto the rocks, striking them, killing them.

Then I'm on the beach, screaming, shaking my fists at them. "What are you doing? These birds are protected! You're breaking the law! Get away from here! Get off the island!"

They look at me as if I'm some kind of psycho. I mash the button on my radio, yell at the dispatcher, my voice cracking, "Emergency, this is an emergency. This is Wheeler up at Hidden Cove. Send someone quick. Get the Park Police up here."

I'm still babbling when the police car roars up the road, blue lights flashing, siren screaming. The officer jumps out of his car and comes at a run.

"They're killing the plovers," I shout, "deliberately chasing and killing them, smashing them with driftwood. I saw him, that ugly kid, where is he? Where has he gone? He deliberately killed a baby plover."

But by then the boys have rounded the ridge of rocks and disappeared. Their manhood proven, they've fled the beach. And the sea has conspired to save them; the tide is busy washing away their footprints.

I walk out among the carnage and begin to count the dead plovers. There are seven. Others may be injured and hidden away.

I look down the beach to where the boys have gone, and I think it's a good thing Geneva gave me only a radio.

On the biggest weekend of the year, the Fourth of July holiday, we get a report that a whale has washed up on the beach north of Gunnison. Geneva and I spin off in the Jeep.

The whale rests partly in the sand, partly in the water. He's gray/black with a white belly and at least 15 feet long. And he's beyond our help. Beyond anyone's help. His back is a mangled mess: a two-foot piece of spine is missing.

"Most likely hit by a boat," Geneva says. She identifies him as a minke, another endangered species. "The bay used to be full of them," she says.

She walks around the dead whale, her hand pressed tight against her mouth and nose. "The propeller nearly cut him in half. Bury him above high tide." She turns and hurries away.

I watch her climb the dune and wonder if what Sallie says is true, that our boss is pregnant.

And how do I get the whale up to where I can bury him? High tide is 50 feet away, up a steep bank.

The old nudie with the three earrings appears from nowhere. "We'll need to cut him in half," he says, shading his eyes from the sun as he looks around, calculating how best to get the job done. "Throw a rope around him and use your Jeep to drag him up past that ledge of rocks. Dig a hole up there and bury him."

"Who is we?" I ask. "And if you want to roam around the island, you'll have to put on some clothes." I end up shouting my final words to his retreating figure.

Ten minutes later he returns with a serrated butcher knife. He's busy sawing through the rubber and fat and torn innards of the minke when I notice he's put on bathing trunks.

It takes me two trips with the Jeep and one ruined clutch before I get both pieces of whale up the hill. I radio for a clean-up crew to come dig the hole.

It'll be morning, at the earliest, before they can come, the guy from maintenance tells me. It might be longer, he says. They'll need a backhoe for the job, and that'll have to come from the mainland.

By then the whale will have ruined many a New Yorker's holiday, I tell him.

I wash off in the ocean, nurse the Jeep down to the parking lot, and return to my job. I find a spot in the dunes where I have a wide view of the beach. I lay my binoculars in the sand, lather on the sun block, spritz on some insect repellent.

The government is paying me thousands of dollars to roam the beaches and look for birds. I am to seek out and protect terns and skimmers, of which there are none.

But I can guard the plovers. Keep people away from their nests. Keep the nudies within their boundaries so they do not offend the sensibilities of the majority.

The old man sits on a nearby rock. I should chase him back to where he belongs, but I do not.

He leans back, looks up at the sky. "I've eaten many a plover egg in my day," he says.

"You've eaten these bird eggs?"

"Sorry, love," he says. "I have."

"My name is Kylie," I tell him.

He talks about ordering the dish in some of the finest restaurants in New York. They were considered a delicacy, he says, looking across the bay toward the city, which is enshrouded in a mantle of pollution. "They served them on toast, covered with Hollandaise. They were mild tasting, kind of like ..." and he gazes up at the sky, searching for a word to describe them.

"People used to come out here to the beaches and collect the eggs," he says. "Stick a needle in them, suck out the insides, and add them to their collections."

Like Geneva with the whale, my stomach has gone queasy.

"It was a long time ago," he says. "We didn't know. Things are so different now. I'm really sorry, little girlie." His eyes seem weary, and his three earrings glint in the sun.

Sailors of long ago wore earrings in case they were lost at sea. If a sailor's body washed up on shore, the hope was that someone would remove the earring and sell it, then use the money to pay for a decent burial.

In the distance I can see the black hulk of the dead whale resting in two parts on top of the hill. Nearby, I see what I think is a fox den, but I choose not to investigate.

The nudie has put on bathing trunks. Things do not fit so neatly anymore.

He calls me "little girlie." I should object to that. Me, Kylie Wheeler. Phi Beta Kappa. Summa Cum Laude. The Bitch who dragged a whale up a hill and tore out a clutch in the process.

But I'm touched. I lean back, close my eyes, scratch the poison ivy blisters on my leg, and think about the fox I rescued. Saved from certain death. Sent to Tennessee where he can cavort with his own.

When I looked through the bars of the cage that day, into the eyes of the fox I'd captured, and he looked at me, I knew I did not want to be the cause of his death.

Now the old man looks at me, and I see that he is old, and gay, and his life has been hard. And there isn't much I can do. Except not make things worse for him. Maybe touch his arm when I leave.

GRID NUMBER FOUR

WHEN I TELL MY CO-WORKERS there are no male squirrels in grid number four, they shrug it off. Scientists that they are, they're unimpressed with the fact that we've captured dozens of females, but not a single male squirrel in more than a month.

"It's meaningless," Stefan says. "A statistical anomaly. Flip a coin a dozen times and it can come up heads every time. But sooner or later, it'll land on tails."

"I knew a family back in Alabama who had nothing but boys," I tell him. "Fourteen boys and not a single girl."

"Next one might have been a girl," he says. "The males are out there, Kylie. Take my word for it." He looks at the folding table we've set up, the equipment we've trucked out from the lodge, the kit squirrel Andy has just anesthetized.

"You can't draw conclusions until all the data has been collected," Stefan says. "You should know that. Biology 101. Basic scientific procedure." He sets off on those long, Abraham Lincoln legs of his, heading out to check his traps.

I watch him disappear, and inside I'm rankling over that Biology 101 crack. My degree is as good as his. I know scientific methodology as well as he.

If he meant the remark for Andy, I'm even more irritated. Stefan and Andy are both graduate students doing research for advanced degrees. They're on equal footing.

"The females in this grid are like Amazons," Andy says, placing the squirrel on the curved tray of our baby scales. "This one could easily top out at two, maybe three pounds when she's grown."

"If she were some other species, maybe. A raccoon or a badger." I squint at the numbers and make a notation on the clipboard. "She weighs seven ounces."

"They use the males, then drive them out," he says. "Just like the American woman."

"You're so cute," I tell him.

"Maybe they're like the praying mantis," Andy says. "They feast on their partners until there's nothing left but back legs and a bit of torso. When the coupling is complete, the male has been all but consumed. He's just twitching legs and a stump of a body."

"Very funny, Andy," I tell him, wondering what on earth I'm doing out here in the middle of this Montana wilderness with these two men.

I take the squirrel off the scales and lay her on the table, ruffling her fur, checking for fleas and other parasites. "She's in good condition. In a few months she'll be all grown up, ready to give some male squirrel a run for his money."

"You're making my case for me," he says.

I hear the smile in his voice, and I wonder if he knows how I feel about him. Does he realize I fell in love with him the first day we met, and each day since has only made me more certain?

"Did you administer the isoflurane?" I ask.

"Two minutes ago," he says.

I glance at the clipboard, see his notation, then look at my watch. It's been exactly two minutes. Did I expect otherwise? I've never worked with anyone who is as meticulous, as dedicated and smart, yet so gentle with the animals in our study.

He attaches electrodes to the squirrel's lips and turns on the machine that will measure the fat content in her body. "Look at those incisors. Did you ever see anything so lethal?"

"You're as bad as Stefan," I tell him, but not believing it for a minute.

Technically, Andy is my boss. The grant that pays his salary is large enough to accommodate an assistant. That's me, Kylie Wheeler, Bachelor of Science degree from the University of Colorado, Boulder, two years out of college, checkered resume.

Some would say I'm floundering. I have no idea what I want to do with the rest of my life. The world is so big, the possibilities endless.

I know I don't want to be a purchasing agent for a data storage facility again. That's what I did right after graduation. When the job morphed from buyer to deflector of bill collectors, I began surfing the web for other opportunities. The Bitterroot Mountains of Montana appeared on my computer screen, but I scrolled on past.

In the spring I laddered out of a helicopter onto the slopes of Mauna Kea in Hawaii. I lived for the next six weeks in a hut at 9,000 feet, searching for the rare poʻouli bird. Struggling to breathe in the thin air, eating packaged food dropped every Saturday from a Cessna Skyhawk, I climbed hills, cut through jungle growth, snapped pictures, and recorded bird songs. It was lonely in that one-room hut built on the side of a volcanic mountain. The nights were full of sounds that kept me awake and sometimes afraid. But the work was important, and I was thrilled with what I was accomplishing.

When my time was finished, I dutifully carried my work product back to the Forestry and Wildlife Headquarters.

They were not pleased. The near-constant rain had damaged the film, and the quality of my recordings was not good. Besides, who would believe the birds were, if not thriving, at least not extinct in that uninhabited, hostile environment? Here's your salary and a ticket back to LAX, honey.

I bought a used Honda Accord and drove across the country, west to east. When the Atlantic Ocean loomed, I stopped. Within a week I had a job as a Park Service Ranger on a barrier island off the coast of New Jersey.

Before I left the island at the end of the summer, I'd buried a minke whale that had been nearly cut in half by a yacht that was plying the waters of New York Harbor. If I contributed to the survival of the piping plover sand birds, the least terns, and the black skimmers that still inhabited that sliver of land, it was incidental. Their environment was so fragile and so uncertain, could anyone really do anything to save them?

The Bitterroot Mountains called again, and this time I answered. I went for an interview, and Andy appeared in my life. I sat in his office at the University of Montana and listened to him describe the project.

Working under the auspices of the University and the National Forest Service, he said, we were to collect information regarding environmental factors which regulate the population density of certain wildlife species, primarily *Lepus americanus* and *Tamiasciurus hudsonicus,* in order to determine the probable outcome of the reintroduction of the *Lynx canadensis* on the existing ecosystem.

I looked at the paper he'd handed me. "Can you tell me exactly what that means?"

He pushed his chair back from the desk, half-crossed his legs, folded his hands around one knee, and he laughed.

"I'm sorry," he said. "The project involves setting up grids in various topographies in order to identify areas best suited for the reintroduction of the Canadian lynx. We'll trap and radio-collar prey animals in the Bitterroot National Forest, specifically, snowshoe hares and red squirrels. We'll collect data relating to diet, disease, litter size, and mortality."

I sat very still and listened, nodding at appropriate moments, looking perplexed at others.

"We'll use the information we collect, from this study and from others that are either going on or have already been completed, to set up mathematical models. When the project is finished, we should be able to predict with near certainty the ultimate success or failure of the reintroduction of the lynx into the area," he said.

He talked on and on, and I tried to listen, but I was enthralled with how the light played on the side of his face, and how the blue of his eyes perfectly matched the blue of his shirt.

"An adult lynx needs two hares or their equivalent every three days in order to survive," he said. "That's why this research is so crucial. What we don't want to happen is to release the lynx and then see them starve to death."

"No," I murmured, shaking my head. His hair was light brown, streaked with blond. I guessed he spent a lot of time outdoors. "No, of course not."

He uncrossed his legs, leaned forward, and put both elbows on his desk. "The most important demographic in determining population persistence will be whether or not the lynx kittens born in the late spring or summer can survive that first winter. They'll be nearly full-grown at that point, but not yet capable of feeding themselves."

He pushed back from the desk, extended his legs, and slid down in the chair. "In order to provide for a litter of two to four kittens, which is the average litter size, the mother has to be a very good hunter. She'll need two to four hares a day to feed her family. But I guess you'd like to hear the specifics of the job?"

I leaned back in my chair. "Yes, please. It sounds interesting."

"We expect this part of the research to last a year, maybe longer. Living facilities will be provided. A stipend of $16,000, transportation, a snowmobile … the living facilities are somewhat sparse, a lodge …"

I looked at the paper in my hand and read the title: Wildlife Biological Science Research Assistant. The jobs I'd had—working for a dot com company, tramping through a rain forest, protecting birds bordering on extinction—I didn't want to do any of that again. This was something new, different from anything I'd ever done before.

I stood up and extended my hand. He took it, held on while he rose from his chair. "So you're interested in the job?" he asked.

I gazed into those cool blue eyes and nodded. "It sounds like what I've been looking for."

Twenty minutes later I walked out of the building, got into my car and drove away. I was on the main highway heading south before I let out a whoop of joy.

The Forest Service Compound is a cluster of weathered log buildings tucked into a narrow valley in the Bitterroot Mountains. Much of the cleared area is in deep shade when I arrive, the sun not yet having climbed high enough to reach the valley floor.

I pull into the parking area in front of the lodge and turn off the engine. Andy comes out onto the porch, descends the steps, and walks toward my car. He's wearing a long-sleeved knit shirt, no jacket.

"This is spectacular," I say, gazing at the snow-capped mountains that surround us. They're so close and they tower so sharply, I expect to hear an echo.

"It's pretty rugged country," he says. "The elevation here is just under 3,000 feet, but the peaks are a lot higher. Come on, I'll show you where you'll be staying."

He helps me carry my belongings into the lodge and up the wooden stairs to the top level. When I'm settled in my room, he suggests a tour of the area. I grab a fleece pullover, and we head out into the wilderness. Our transportation is an old GMC truck.

"Think you can learn to drive this thing?" he asks. "It's a stick shift." The motor growls as he pulls out onto the highway.

"So is my Honda," I tell him.

"You need four-wheel drive to get to most of the places we'll be going. The roads aren't much more than old logging trails. This truck is pretty much our only transportation up into the higher grids. Later on, when the snows come, we'll use the snowmobile to get around."

The grids are not what I expected. I'd imagined perfect squares, something akin to an archaeological dig I'd once seen in Mobile Bay. These are large plots of land, each containing 25 acres. Grid number one is a combination of grassland, shrubs, and new-growth saplings. The highway cuts through this grid; it has the lowest elevation and is closest to our lodge. Two is filled with prairie grasses and ponderosa pine. Three is a fertile valley containing a mixture of Douglas fir, spruce, and lodge pole pine. Four has gentle hills, a meandering brook that winds down into grid three, stands of cotton-wood trees on both sides of the water. Five is a steep hillside with several fast-running mountain streams. Six is a high alpine area.

We're coming down a hill through grid number five when Andy suddenly pulls to the side of the road, cuts the engine, and grabs a set of binoculars from the glove compartment.

"Look over there, Kylie. Do you see him? In front of that stand of trees? It's a wolf. No radio collar. He's wild-born, you can bet on it."

We get out of the truck, and Andy raises the glasses. The air is cold, but I breathe in great gulps of it.

"I wish I'd brought a dart gun," he says.

"You'd anesthetize him? Why?" The wolf moves slowly along the hillside.

"So I could put a collar on him."

"But wolves aren't part of the research."

"Not specifically, but he's a predator. If he's a member of a pack, that could have an enormous impact on the eco-system. If he's a disperser, then he could be gone tomorrow. A radio-telemetry collar would tell us that." He hands me the binoculars and leans against the truck fender. "Here, take a look."

I scan the hillside, but the wolf has disappeared. I can find no trace of him.

"The more we learn about predator-prey relationships," Andy says, "the less likely we'll be to intervene, to try to control nature when we shouldn't. It isn't always a pretty picture, but there's a balance out there, and if we upset that balance, at some point we'll pay the price. Do you realize we've eliminated nearly all the predator species that used to live in these mountains?

"With wolves, if we can understand things like the social dynamic within a pack, what it takes for them to survive, the size of their territory, how they kill, what they kill, causes of mortality, we can correct some of the misconceptions we have about them. The same with the lynx. If we can ever get to the point where we're able to restore some sort of balance, we might actually improve the environment. Both for us and for other species."

"But if you put a collar on him, isn't that an intervention? Won't that change his behavior?"

He shrugs. "He'd get used to it. In no time at all he'd forget he was wearing it."

We get back in the truck and he sits for a time, hands on the steering wheel, looking straight ahead. "If we can only learn to appreciate the complexity of the ecosystem, and the part that each species plays in it, maybe then we can begin to let nature regulate herself." He sits for a moment longer. Then he starts the engine, and we resume our journey down the mountain.

I catch a glimpse of the wolf before we turn into a switch-back. He's standing in a copse of trees, head raised, sniffing the air.

We bait the Havahart traps and set them out in the evening, check them in the morning. At times we capture a dozen or more animals in a single day, other times only a few.

Each newly-trapped animal must be anesthetized, examined, weighed, radio-collared, and released back into the wild.

I'd been there for nearly six weeks when we noticed the discrepancy between the ratio of male vs. female squirrels in grid four. The squirrel on our table is another in the string of females we've captured. Where are the males, I wonder?

The kit begins to stir, dislodging one of the electrodes.

"She's so young," I tell Andy. "I doubt there's an ounce of fat on her."

He nods but reattaches the electrode. He watches the dial for a minute, then removes her from the machine. No measurable fat content.

I fasten the collar around her neck while Andy enters the information in our logbook. When he's finished, he returns the squirrel to her cage and begins to load our equipment onto the bed of the truck.

When we reach the grid, I carry the cage away from the road and place it by a deep thicket. Though I see no evidence of predators, I shove the cage back into the brush until it's almost completely hidden. I open the door and step to the side. She's still too sleepy to move.

The noise of the truck will frighten her if she's close to consciousness when Andy starts the engine. At some point she'll awaken and look around. The collar will feel strange, and she'll shake her head, trying to rid herself of the alien thing.

When she's calm and acclimated to this new place, and when all is quiet once again, she'll venture out and scamper off. That's what I choose to believe, though I know her world is full of predators, and it may not be true.

On our walk-through several days later, we find an adult squirrel trapped in one of our grid four cages. There's no sound on our radio-receiver, so we know we've either caught a new animal, or the collar has failed.

Andy kneels by the cage. "It's a male," he says. "We've finally caught one."

"Shoots your Amazon theory, doesn't it?" I catch a whiff of the peanut butter we smeared on the trip wire the day before.

"He's probably been here all along. He just managed to elude us," Andy says.

I might suggest that the males are smarter than the females, more suspicious of our traps, but I don't want to make his argument for him again.

A bit of isoflurane-soaked cotton on a stick, waved under his nose, and he goes limp. I take him out of the cage and place him on the scales. He's a large specimen, his coat richly red, his tail long and bushy. He weighs well over a pound.

"No food shortage here. He's getting his share of pine cones and then some." I hold the sleeping animal up, look into his face. "He's so cute, we should take a picture. I have a camera in my backpack."

Andy administers the anesthesia that will keep the squirrel snoozing, and I run back to the truck for my camera.

He's still asleep, collared, and curled up on a sunny rock when I return. The lighting is perfect and I snap several pictures. Wanting a different pose, I find a pine cone on the ground. I prop him up, and when I try to place the pine cone between his paws, I realize he's not breathing. I grab him up, thump on his chest, feel for a heartbeat.

"Andy," I cry, "come help. He's not breathing."

Andy grabs the squirrel from me, blows into his face, short, fast breaths, trying to get fresh air into his lungs, hoping to reduce the effect of the anesthesia.

It's no use. We can't revive him.

The only male squirrel we've trapped in grid number four is dead.

Andy lays him on the rock and curls his tail around him. A light wind ruffles his fur, and I smooth it down, noting how well groomed and soft it is. His body seems smaller now. I gaze off into the forest, wondering if there are females out there who will have his babies. In the spring of the year will the woods be alive with the chattering of his kits grown to adulthood?

I wonder if Andy and I will still be together in the spring. Or will we go our separate ways, the project abandoned, Andy's dream of restoring some semblance of balance to this ecosystem frustrated?

Stefan is discouraged. He's been back to the University and returned with a stack of newspapers. A firestorm of publicity has erupted. The papers feature articles describing our project and the ultimate goal of the research. Opposition is fierce, and it is building.

It is unlikely that the lynx will ever be re-introduced into this part of the country, Stefan says. The ranchers will never allow it. Predator species that once threatened their livestock—wolves, coyotes, bear, mountain lions—have been all but eradicated. Now the government is spending taxpayer money on programs that could lead to the reintroduction and repopulation of some of these predators. Though the lynx pose no threat to livestock, cattlemen see their possible reintroduction as a victory for environmentalists, one that will lead to financial loss, and ultimately, disaster for their industry. They're complaining to every elected official they can find, in Billings, Missoula, Bozeman, and Washington, D.C.

Federal money has been appropriated, studies designed, personnel hired and placed in the field, data accumulated, but the reason for it all is whirling down to the bottom of a political sea.

The death of the anesthetized squirrel is not an isolated incident. It happens again and again that summer. Andy broods about it nearly as much as I do. "What are we doing wrong?" he wonders.

We recheck the guidelines, reduce the amount of time needed for our exams, adjust the dosage.

"We'll figure this out," he insists. "There's some variable at work here, something we're missing."

I see the concern on his face, and I wish it were spring again. What happened to the light-hearted banter that went on between us back then?

I'm in the lodge kitchen one afternoon when I hear Andy talking on the phone. "I'm wondering if there's another anesthesia we might try," he says. "The dosage seems to be so critical ..." He's talking to our project director at the University. Coffee mug in hand, I walk into the dining area of the great room.

"… it's such a small window, there's no room for error. If we misjudge, the animal dies."

I lean against the wall and sip my coffee, watching him. I'm close enough that I can hear the voice on the other end of the line.

"Isoflurane was chosen because it wears off quickly, and the animal can be released back into the environment," his professor says. "It's a powerful agent, Andy. You have to expect some mortalities."

Andy nods. "I wonder if it might skew our results."

"I wouldn't worry about it," comes the answer. "Not unless your mortalities reach a significant number. They're rodents, Andy. Food for coyotes, foxes, bears, eagles, and ultimately, the lynx."

Andy hangs up the phone and turns away. I walk back to the kitchen. In a few minutes, I hear the outside door close behind him.

Andy's view of the world is different from mine. He believes passionately in the re-introduction of predatory animals into the environment. He looks at the ecology of the whole Northwest. His mission is to restore the balance that has been disrupted by man.

I see a squirrel that died because we overdosed him.

The Canadian lynx is a rare and beautiful animal, brought to near extinction for its fur, for sport, for machismo. One cat in the wilderness, stretched out on a tree limb, watching the forest floor, is a thing of such power and majesty, who would deny him his sustenance? Snowshoe hares, red

squirrels, and terrestrial birds: all are part of the food chain.
Our work here in the Bitterroot Mountains is at the bottom
of that chain. Humans are at the top. I shouldn't care if some
of the animals die. But I do.

I pour out the rest of my coffee and watch it swirl down
the drain. It leaves a dark stain on the white porcelain.

It seems unusually quiet in the forest as autumn settles over
the land. The maple tree outside my bedroom window changes
color overnight, and the light that comes into the room is filtered gold. The change is so surprising and so marked, I turn
off my alarm clock and lie in a pocket of warmth beneath
the quilt for an extra ten minutes. In this cold land that will
soon be colder than anything I have ever experienced, I feel
safe and warm.

The days are shorter now, and the work less intensive.
Andy and I often go separately to the grids. I walk through
the woods, setting the traps, checking them, gathering the
data. I come across squirrels and bunnies I know by habit
and sometimes by name.

It is not sad when I find animals that have died, even ones
I've recently collared. Snowshoe hares are occasionally killed
on the highway. Squirrels are taken by predators. Sometimes
I find a collar that has gone silent. When I check the numbers,
I can identify which animal has died. Often I have no way
of determining what happened to the animal. It is simply
gone. I can deal with that. What's hard is when what we've
done has resulted in an injury or a mortality.

One crisp autumn morning I catch a glimpse of a grid three squirrel we trapped early in the summer. She's blind in one eye, so she's easy to identify.

When we first found her in the cage back in June, she was a bloody mess. Somehow she'd managed to get her head through one of the squares in the trap. There must have been a loose piece of wire; in her fright she thrashed around, and the wire did its damage. Andy always keeps wire cutters in the truck, so we were able to get her out without doing more harm. I cleaned her up, did what I could for her. I wanted to take her back to the lodge and keep her for a time, but Andy believed she'd be better off in the wild. So we released her.

A week later I thought I saw her jumping through the trees, but I wasn't certain. Now I am. It's the same squirrel. The eye is milky white, but she's survived. She's functioning, even thriving. I can't wait to tell Andy.

Yet there's a sadness about it. Seeing her sitting on that limb reminds me of the chattering, rustling sounds of summer. The woods back then were a Garden of Eden. But no more.

I wonder if I should have walked away from that sun-bleached rock where I snapped the picture of the sleeping squirrel. Winter is approaching. Soon it will no longer be possible to leave. The Arctic winds will blast across the border, icing the Montana landscape, and I'll be stuck. There will be no escape. The sadness, the viciousness of nature, the knowledge of how helpless we are to affect a change, it will come crashing down on me.

A cold front sweeps down from the north and lingers for several days. The three of us gather in the lodge each evening to drink reconstituted hot chocolate and talk about our project. The pine timbers in the ceiling and walls are dark with smoke from the stone fireplace; the room smells of the hundreds of fires kept burning through the long winter months.

In October Stefan announces that his work with the hares is nearly finished. For the next two weeks he'll need as much help as Andy and I can give him. Thirty bunnies must be captured, killed, frozen, and shipped back to the University. There they will be fed into a machine that will grind them up, whirl them around with such centrifugal force that fat will be separated from bone and other tissue.

This final phase is necessary in order to check the validity of all the data we've gathered since spring.

Andy will finish his part of the project shortly thereafter. He will sacrifice an equal number of red squirrels. Then he will head back to the University to complete the next phase of the research.

I am to stay through the winter. The focus of the work will shift to a study of the dietary needs of the snowshoe hare. Can they survive on the measured bits of cedar and grand fir I am to feed them? How will they be affected by being forced to eat things they would never eat in the wild?

The fire alternately crackles and roars, and the new kid hired to care for the Forest Service horses comes in.

"Close the door," Stefan yells. The boy has to strain to pull it shut against a tearing wind.

Bone thin, he looks to be no more than seventeen or eighteen. He smooths his windswept blond hair down over his forehead, attempting to cover a face littered with acne. He makes a cup of hot chocolate and sits on the floor in front of the fire.

The hermit who lives in a cabin by one of the mountain streams comes in. He's found one of our traps out by the highway. Afraid it might be stolen, he's hidden it in a clump of grass.

Like most outdoorsmen, it's hard to tell his age. His hair is dark, his face deeply tanned. The wrinkles around his eyes and mouth tell me he's at least 60, maybe older.

He's heard that I'm taking a creative writing course from the University of Colorado. He wants me to read the autobiography he's writing. It's 2,000 pages long, but he's only brought 800 of them with him.

He removes the manuscript from his shoulder bag and hands it to me, and I notice that his hand trembles.

The manuscript is hand-written on college-ruled notebook paper, the writing so tiny I wonder how I can possibly read it without a magnifying glass. I take the stack of papers and tell him I'll be happy to read it.

The new hire drinks his chocolate and talks about the herd of moose that came out of the woods this morning. "They were milling around in the pasture behind the barn," he says. "Must have been a dozen of them. There's one old bull that followed me all around, everywhere I went. Pawed the ground, like he was gonna attack."

"Maybe he was interested in your horse," Stefan says.

The boy frowns.

"Don't worry, he won't bother you. Just leave him alone."

"He's probably hungry," Andy says. "There's not much out there for him to eat this time of year. Throw him some grain."

"I'm gonna buy a tag tomorrow," the boy says. "I'm not taking any chances."

He lays down his $12 the next day and gets his tag. He now has official permission from the state of Montana to kill one bull moose.

Which he does. That afternoon I see the horse, laboring up from the pasture, dragging the dead moose behind him. The boy's blue heeler is running beside the horse. The dog looks scared. As if he wishes he were anywhere else but where he is.

A gust of wind lifts the boy's blonde hair off his forehead. There's no room for another zit.

The days pass, and each one folded up and put away is a step closer to what is about to happen. Thirty squirrels and a like number of snowshoe hares will give their lives for science. For the advancement of knowledge. A sacrifice for the betterment of mankind.

There are days of reasoned discussion among the three of us, and evenings of heated arguments in the cathedral-ceilinged great room of the lodge. The weather turns frigid, the temperature dropping into the single digits at night. The windows in my room are white with frost.

Before the first heavy snowfall, Andy and I go out together to pre-bait three of the grids. Because he's been so involved in the mathematical projections that flow from the grid system, I've come to know the forest better than he does. I can identify many of the nesting trees.

"No sense baiting this tree," I tell him. "The squirrel is gone."

"Another one will take over his territory in the spring," Andy says.

We walk through an area that is heavily wooded and thick with undergrowth. When we find active middens, pine cones piled beneath limbs of trees, we bait the trees and move on.

The next morning we check the traps and release the squirrels that have already been collared. There are no new catches, and I'm glad.

Andy notices. "I'm sorry, Kylie. I know how much this bothers you. But there's no other way. If the research we've done is to have any value, I have to complete this final step. It will not only provide verification of the data already collected, but also information regarding the nutritional value of the prey species we're studying. Ultimately, we'll be able to predict with a fair degree of accuracy whether a predator species like the lynx will be able to survive."

He stops and looks at me. "Stefan and I will handle it," he says. "You don't have to be there. If you'll just keep on with the regular work, we'll do the rest."

"Tell me about the machine," I ask.

"It's called a centrifugal separator."

"How does it work?"

"It separates the fat from other tissue."

I wait for him to go on, but he doesn't. There's no need. A snowshoe hare that is getting plenty to eat, building layers of fat, provides more nutritional value than one that is starving. Squirrels that are thriving will have more kits, many of which will become food for predators that roam the countryside.

We walk on, moving away from the forest into the meadow cut through by the stream. He wants me to stay through the winter. He plans to visit every few weeks to check on the condition of the snowshoe hares I'll be studying in this new phase of the research.

"Have you noticed the bunnies are turning colors?" I ask. "Stefan caught one the other day that was almost pure white."

"Camouflage," he says. "Brown in the summer, white in the winter. Did you give him a name?"

He knows me too well.

We circle back through the forest and return to the lodge. We load a dozen cages into the bed of the Park Service truck and drive to grid five.

It matters to him what I think, he says. It matters a great deal.

We take the cages off the truck and carry them into the grid.

"We'll do it in the most humane way possible," he says. "The animals will be anesthetized. Identified, weighed, and measured. Overdosed. Placed in the lodge freezer, then shipped to the University."

"How much do they have invested in this machine?" I ask. "This centrifugal separator? Is that the reason for all this? They spent a million dollars for this fancy new machine, and now they have to justify it? They have to find some use for it, so they can answer to their Board of Directors?"

"I don't think that's it," he says.

I look at him, kneeling there on the ground, carefully setting the mechanism that will trip the cage door.

I leave him. I walk out of the forest, past the truck, down the logging road to the highway. On the macadam I pick up an easy jog. The air is cold in my lungs, but in a few minutes I'm used to it, and I keep going.

The lodge is at least ten miles away. I've never jogged that far. But this evening it seems possible.

I'm an Aztec runner charged with delivering a message from the tribal leader in Mexico City to the tribal leader in Acapulco. When I reach that city, 180 miles away, I will hand over the message. Then I will drop dead, my heart having burst in my chest.

It's dark when I get back to the compound. Andy is waiting for me.

"I'll stay," I tell him. "There's nowhere else I want to go."

"Good," he says. "I'm glad." He puts his arms around me and pulls me close, and I lay my head against his chest. I breathe in the smell of him.

"I'll be lonely here without you," I tell him.

"I'll come back as often as I can," he says.

Nothing stirs in winter that does not have to stir. At night I hear the traffic out on the highway, but mostly the woods are silent.

The killing is done. Stefan packed his belongings and returned to the University. Andy left a few days later. There's time to sit by the fire during the long evenings, to think about what's happened, and to wonder what lies ahead.

The research on the winter diets of snowshoe hares is more benign than what has gone before. Stefan has left a dozen white bunnies caged behind the lodge. In the spring I will release them back into the wild.

My job is to care for the hares over the winter. I am to dole out measured amounts of specific foods. I will feed, water, weigh, observe, and document. Conditions permitting, I will visit the grids and record wildlife sightings. I am to recover any collars that have begun a rapid beep, an indication that the animal has not moved for several hours and is likely dead. The collars each cost over $200, Stefan reminded me before he left. "Load up the snowmobile, go out into the grids, and recover any you can find," he said.

The snow falls steadily, sometimes for days on end. In the mountains even the tallest of the firs are up to their knees in snow. The land is white and black.

Inside the lodge the fire is warm. The boy who killed the moose keeps the north section of the porch filled with seasoned wood. Now that I'm here alone, he rarely comes into the lodge.

The shelves in the pantry are filled with Campbell's soups, canned vegetables, potted meats, fruit juices, Carnation milk, dried fruits, and pasta. The freezer is empty.

Occasionally I hear the thump of snow sliding off the branches of a tree, the roar of some distant avalanche sliding down the mountains, the grumble of snowplows working around the clock to keep the highway and back roads open.

There's time to begin reading the manuscript left by the hermit, and to catch up on the creative writing course I'm taking.

The hermit's story begins with a recurring dream that has bedeviled him for as long as he can remember. He's caught beneath a building that has collapsed around him. He's lying on a dirt floor. The space around him is small. He can barely move. When he tries to rise, he cannot. He sees a flicker of light in the distance. It's small, the size of a foundation vent, but it's an opening. He begins to crawl toward it, but he knows the opening is too small. His head will never fit. If by some miracle he's able to get his head free, his shoulders will never make it. Still, he wriggles forward.

Like David Copperfield, the hermit has begun the story of his life at the beginning of his life. I read on for twenty pages or so, then lay the manuscript aside.

The room has chilled. I get up from the couch, pile logs on the fire, and turn to the creative writing course. My assignment is to read a speech delivered by Elie Wiesel a number of years ago and to write an essay.

Wiesel spoke of violence in the 20th century, of the Great War that was surely the last war that would ever be fought. Twenty million people died. Then came the second Great War, and this time the toll is more uncertain. Thirty million? Fifty million? Then Korea, Vietnam, Kosovo, Kuwait, Iraq, Afghanistan, Iraq again. The locations change or do not change, but the wars go on.

The wind howls outside the lodge and the fallen snow is restless.

Once the hermit loved a horse, and the horse died. He was alone. There was no one to help him. With only a shovel, a pickaxe, and a come-along, he managed to dig a grave and to bury the horse. He never wanted another.

He told that story back in the summer, when we were all sitting on the porch of the lodge.

The wind sweeps down the sharp inclines of the mountain and curls around the edges of the buildings. Snow swirls against the tall windows of the lodge. A sudden gust sends a puff of ashes into the room where I sit. The fire sputters.

I get up from the couch, adjust the flue, and replace the fireplace screen. The fire returns to a steady burn.

A siren out on the highway sets off the coyotes, and the night is no longer silent. The coyotes sing their high-quavering songs, as if in sympathy for the person being transported: injured motorist, heart attack victim, gunshot rancher. Their howls taper off into yelping, barking, yipping.

For a time it is quiet. Then the howling begins again, without provocation this time, a cacophony of sounds as if all the coyotes in the whole preserve are gathered outside my door.

There are other sounds. Sounds that are not coyote. An animal is screaming, fighting for its life. I walk to the window, praying it will end quickly. It goes on and on and on. Finally, it is finished.

I should go outside and check on the snowshoe hares. Their cages are set in an alcove beside the building where we house the truck and other equipment. Could one of the bunnies have escaped and become a meal for a pack of hungry coyotes? I've already lost three of the original twelve. Two died and one escaped. I can't lose anymore.

But if I went outside, what could I do?

The hearth stones radiate heat into the room long after the fire is only glowing embers. The snow has stopped, the wind calmed for the night. I sit with the manuscript in my lap, wondering about the hermit and other living things out in that frigid darkness.

In the morning I'll move the bunnies. They need to be in an environment more like the one from which we took them. There's a cluster of spruce trees near the road that leads out to the highway. I'll take them there.

When I open the lodge door in the morning, I'm careful to make no sound, but still the bunnies hear. They begin to thump, warning each other of danger, then to scream. Before I come into view, they are screaming with fear and despair. It's been nearly a month; will they never get used to me, never learn to trust me?

Stefan's car is parked near the cages. He's driven down from the University to pick up the two mortalities.

"We'll have to do necropsies," he says. "We need to know why they died."

"They're starving to death," I tell him. "They don't like what I'm feeding them. They won't eat it."

"They'll eat it," he answers. "They just need to get hungry enough. We have to follow the protocol that's been set up."

Stefan is a scientist. He does not let emotion taint his clear-thinking brain.

"I'm sorry about the one that got away."

"It's okay," he says.

"Is Andy planning to come down?"

"He might try to break away this weekend. I don't know. I haven't seen much of him lately." He wraps the dead bunnies in a towel and puts them in the trunk of his car. "It could be stress," he says. "Or disease. We'll have to wait until we get the results. I'll let you know."

"If the necropsy shows they died of malnutrition, can we change the diet?"

"We're about to change it anyway," he says. "That's the next stage of the research."

Ultimately the research should determine the factors that regulate the hare population. Cover, availability of food, and predation are part of the equation, but they do not account for the unexplained crashes in the hare population that happen from time to time. Should one of these crashes occur after the reintroduction of the lynx, the project will fail.

That afternoon I begin moving the cages. I close my ears to the screaming and I drag them, one by one, into the spruce-enclosed area. My hope is that in this new location they'll feel safe. It is as close as I can come to an environment that is like the grids where they once lived.

While I work I talk to them, and I'm careful to keep my voice soft and melodic. I call them by the names I've given them. They're silly names. Hoppie, Skippy, and Lou, remnants of some nursery rhyme that ran though my head when Stefan was putting them in their cages. Peggy, for her lame foot. Buddy, a big rangy rabbit who looks like a drunken hillbilly. Tom, for Thomas Wolfe, one of my favorite authors. Thoreau, for the thoughtful way he looks at me. Blackfoot, with one dark foot that never whitens and because I need an Indian in the bunch. And Joseph, for Joseph Smith, the Mormon, who had a long face like this hare. Joseph seems such a serious type.

I would like for this Joseph to have many wives, like his namesake, but I doubt it will happen.

Both Tom, the writer, and Joseph, the founder of a religion, are dying. They are not able to survive on the diet I am feeding them. When I put the food into their cages, they move as far away from me as the cage will allow. Sometimes I see them nibbling on the cedar chips, but their intake is negligible. Joseph's eyes, once bright and clear, are cloudy and dull. Tom trembles when I approach his cage. The tenor of his scream has changed. It no longer sounds like the cry of a frightened baby. It is like keening.

If they were free, they would not be eating cedar and grand fir. Even in the harshest of winters they would find food more to their liking. They could feast on strips of bark, twigs, buds, and pine needles. The higher grids have lodge pole pine and subalpine fir. They would have plenty to eat, if they were in one of the higher grids. They could have eating orgies, like ancient Romans. They could set up a vomitorium where they could go to regurgitate, then go back and eat some more.

If they die, I can't even bury them. I have to turn their bodies over to science. Stomach contents are important to scientists.

The snowplows run continuously. When the main highway has been scraped and salted, the road crews start on the secondary roads, pushing the snow to the sides, piling it up. Double lanes thin to single lanes. The paths through the snow banks begin to resemble tunnels. When I take the Park Service truck up into the grids, snowmobile loaded on the trailer, often I can see only a thin swath of sky directly above me.

Cabin fever threatens to overwhelm me, so I go to the grids several times a week, to record conditions, document wildlife sightings, determine the cause of death of collared animals, and retrieve collars. Mostly I go to breathe the fresh air.

Out in the grids the world seems a peaceful place. Except for the hum of semis on the highway, the wind, the tree branches that crack under the weight of snow, it's quiet in the mountains. I close my ears to the occasional gunshot or the smattering of gunshots that break the silence.

I'm searching for a radio collar that's broadcasting in mortality mode when I see the remnants of the moose harem. Once there were a dozen members. Now there are only five. They mill around the stream that runs through the meadow, munching twigs and shrubs that grow along the water.

The bull moose is gone. Head mounted on a cabin wall, rug on a cabin floor. What happened to the others, I wonder? Has the boy who killed the bull developed a taste for killing? Is it possible the herd could have been decimated by wolves? There's no evidence of a pack, no reason to believe the lone wolf we saw in the spring was anything other than a disperser driven out from his pack.

I leave the moose and take the snowmobile up to grid five where I fill a gunny sack with branches from lodge pole pine and subalpine fir. No more cedar and grand fir; the diet has finally been changed. The bunnies are thriving in their new, spruce home, their favorite foods prepared and delivered by their own personal chef, fresh water provided twice a day, cages cleaned daily.

The hermit tells me they'll never survive. The months of captivity will have dulled their survival instincts, he says. Predators will grab them an hour after you've released them. Coyote, fox, great-horned owl, weasel, bobcat; their enemies are many. Your bunnies are doomed, he says.

He comes often to the lodge that winter, as if some remnant of chivalry lives on in him.

"Would you object if I shoveled the walk for you, a path out to the garage?" he asks after a heavy snowfall. I smile at his choice of words, pick up both shovels that are propped against the lodge wall, and hand one to him. Together we work for most of the afternoon.

One day he brings me a freshly-killed rabbit. He holds the pink carcass out to me, as if offering a gift. Again I notice the tremor in his hand.

I demur.

"It was killed on the road," he says.

I nod, aware that I've crossed my arms against him and his gift. I uncross them, but shake my head again.

He sighs and looks toward the mountains, then stuffs the carcass back into his game pouch.

"The kid didn't do such a good job with the wood," he says, eyeing the stack of firewood at the north end of the porch. "I could split some for you. It would be no trouble."

"I have just over a hundred pages of your manuscript left. I could read it while you work." I see a flicker of pleasure in his dark eyes.

When he takes his manuscript back that afternoon, he leaves me with another, this one no more than twenty pages. "It's a true story," he says, "about a wolf named Rags the Digger. When you've read it, you'll understand the nature of man."

"Is this some deep philosophical treatise?" I ask. "A biblical story with a universal application and a great moral lesson?"

He only smiles. "Just a story that's been told around a few hundred campfires over the years."

"While wolves howled in the background?"

"Coyotes, more likely," he says. "I want you to read it," and he hands it to me. "It will all come together for you. The essay you wrote about Elie Wiesel, your young man Andy, and a bounty hunter who lived a long time ago. Throw in a touch of Henry David Thoreau. And a bit of me. Cornelius Devny Morain."

"I know who you are," I answer. "I read the first section of your autobiography, remember? And loved every word of it."

"You are a beautiful child, Kylie."

"So are you, Cornelius Devny Morain."

"Why Thoreau?" I ask, an afterthought, having already turned away from him.

"You'll understand when you've read it," he says. He adjusts the strap of his shoulder bag and walks away. I do not see him again.

I take the snowmobile down to the spot where I parked the truck, throw my bag of pine branches onto the passenger seat, and head for the compound.

All those pages of his autobiography, laboriously written in that tiny script, and I have no real understanding of why this man chose to live apart. The great sweep of his life had been lost in the details of it.

Spring is approaching. There are days when the temperature climbs above freezing and the sun bores down onto the white earth. Trees have begun to cast off their mantles of snow. Mountain streams are beginning to trickle. Ice is melting, cracking, breaking loose. Patches of gravel have begun to emerge from under the snow and ice.

Andy is driving down this weekend. It's time to begin releasing the bunnies, he says.

I pull the Park Service truck off the side of the mountain road near grid four, cut the engine, and set the emergency brake. Patches of snow are still visible in shady areas, but the day is warm and clear.

Joseph in his Havahart cage on the back of the truck believes he has breathed his last. He trembles at the sight of me. He has probably been trembling all the way up the mountain.

I approach him slowly, talking to him, saying nonsensical things I would not want anyone to hear, hoping he will not scream that awful scream. We are alone on the side of a mountain, this snowshoe hare and I, and I am about to set him free after months of captivity.

He's recovered from his awful lethargy and his terrible thinness, though he has built up no reserves. I've fed him the twisted needles of the lodge pole pine, the succulent branches of Douglas fir, twigs and bits of bark. He no longer screams when I approach him. But he is not at the top of his game. The muscles he needs to survive have clearly atrophied.

Joseph with the long face, I hope that soon you can run as fast as you did in the fall. I hope you find many wives out there. I hope you are not dispatched before your natural time.

I let down the tailgate. He leaps, crashing into the back of his cage. Blood spurts down his chest; he has reopened an old wound. I slide the cage forward and lift it from the truck bed.

There's nothing I can do about the blood or his injured nose. When it first happened back in the winter, the injury turned dark and crusted over, and it seemed a terrible thing against his whiteness. Now he has begun to turn camouflage brown, and I hope the injury will heal. I lift the cage off the truck bed and carry it into the woods.

The pounding of his heart when I picked him up earlier today was so fast, it seemed to be one great pulsating beat without interval. Working as quickly as I could, expecting that he might die of fright at any moment, I weighed and collared him, then put him in his traveling cage.

There's no way to tell a wild animal you mean him no harm. He has survived all the tests devised for him. The results have been set down on learned papers at the University of Montana, submitted in triplicate to the heads of the Biology Department, the National Park Service, the Department of the Interior, and who knows else. I have done what they asked. Lowly Biological Science Research Assistant that I am, I have followed their instructions to the letter. Now he will go free.

I carry the cage far into the grid, looking for the best place to release him.

I don't know if any of the hares I have cared for these long months will survive. The level of stress they have experienced has been monumental, perhaps toxic. They may not be able to adjust to freedom.

This I do know: they have escaped the certain death of the isoflurane-impregnated wick. They have managed to live on the scant rations I've fed them over the winter. The information I've gathered concerning their nutritional needs sits in a file somewhere back at the University. The God of Knowledge has been fed, though he is hungry still. The collars will, for a time, provide still more data. Then my work will be finished.

Grid five has scant vegetation. Will the bunnies I plan to release tomorrow have a better chance of survival in that grid, where there is so little to eat and so few places to hide? Or is this grid with its tangled vegetation and tall trees and rushing waters a more hospitable place? Grid five has few predators; four has many. Coyotes and birds of prey tend to cruise the grids where meals are more plentiful.

I look for a place to release Joseph where he will have the best chance of survival. There are trees, tufts of dead grass, some pale new growth, a thin trickle of water from beneath a rock.

I set the cage down near a ponderosa pine that rises out of a cold snow bank. It's a good place. He'll have water and his favorite food. I open the door and he shoots out of the enclosure. He bounds toward the west in great leaps and then veers north.

Maybe he'll survive. Maybe he'll come back to the tree and the snow bank. Maybe not. Maybe the bunnies I plan to release tomorrow in grid five will be able to find enough food to survive.

I walk out of the woods and sling the empty cage into the back of the truck. I get in the cab and crank the engine. Nothing happens. A faint clicking noise at first, then nothing.

Damn. I pound the steering wheel. Corroded battery post? It happened once before, back in the fall.

Motorist in trouble, an upraised hood, someone stops. This is Montana. I get out of the truck, pop the hood, and within ten minutes I have company.

It's a man and a boy coming up the mountain in a shiny new Toyota Tacoma.

"Need some help?" the man asks. He's Texas tall, wearing jeans and a flannel shirt.

"I think it's my battery," I tell him.

"Get the jumpers out of the toolbox," he tells the boy.

The kid is smooth-faced, twelve or thirteen. A roll of belly hangs over his silver-conched belt.

The man attaches the red and black cables, signals to the boy in the Toyota to start the engine. He climbs into my truck, turns the key. The starter grinds, but the motor fails to catch. The boy revs the Toyota, to no avail. The man gets out of the truck, removes his hat, dusts his trouser legs, finger-combs his hair, returns the hat.

"It shoulda started if it was the battery. Must be something else wrong with it. We can give you a lift," he says.

"I'm heading down to the Park Service compound. The opposite direction. I can walk. It's just a few miles."

"We could turn your truck around. You could coast down most of the way."

"I think I'll walk. It's not too far."

Back at the compound, I locate a ball of steel wool and head back toward the truck. Coca-Cola will eat away corrosion on battery posts, I've heard, but it can take hours. Who even has a Coca-Cola, out here in this wilderness? The sun is sinking toward the horizon.

I jog up Bitterroot Mountain and set to work on the battery post, scratching away at the crunchy white residue that has accumulated. When I turn the key in the ignition, the truck belches blue smoke, shakes herself on loose motor mounts, and cranks. I do a tight u-turn between the walls of snow on both sides of the road. I head toward home, nursing her around the curves, expecting her to conk out at any moment. She'll need a thousand dollar stay in the hospital before I'll trust her again. I suspect she has more problems than corroded battery connections. Alternator, maybe.

I take her through the switchbacks down the mountain, thinking of Grace Kelly in the south of France, wondering if the mountain road where she was killed was anything like this one. She would have been driving some fancy car, a Jaguar or a BMW. Maybe a Peugeot. Not an old rusty heap like this that belongs in a junk yard.

A quarter mile down the mountain I see the Toyota again, parked by the side of the road. I slow down. I hear what sounds like a gunshot. I pull in behind the truck.

Another shot rings out. I jump out of the truck and take off running, pushing through dense vegetation. More predators come to this grid than any of the others.

More than I imagined. Father and son stand in a grove of lodge pole pine. Each has a gun. They are taking turns shooting at something in the woods.

"I got it started," I tell them, eyeing the guns. "I used some steel wool to clean off the connections. What are you shooting at?"

"It shoulda started, if it was the battery. I'd have it checked out." The man props his gun against a tree and leans back, his knee bent. "Just shooting," he adds. "Doin' some target practice."

The boy aims along the length of his rifle and fires. The shot is close to the ground: I see a puff of dust and cringe. Does this kid know about ricochet?

"You got him," the father says.

The kid runs into the woods. He comes back carrying a squirrel by the tail. He tosses it to the ground by my feet.

"Target practice? You're shooting squirrels for the fun of it?" I pick up the animal from the ground where the boy dropped him. "Do you realize this is a Columbia ground squirrel?

He's been hibernating all winter long, and he's managed to survive, and you come along and kill him?"

"We're just practicing," the boy says. "I'm a pretty good shot."

"You call this good? To kill an animal for no reason? Do you know he's been in a hole in the ground, and he's stayed hidden away from martens, and he didn't starve to death, and now he comes out, and he's hardly awake, and you kill him?"

"Martens? One of those nasty weasel things? Be fun to shoot one of them."

"Do you even hear what I'm saying?"

"Are you a tree hugger?" the boy asks, and I want to smack his face for his ignorance and his arrogance.

"We study squirrels and snowshoe hares in this grid. Haven't you seen the collars we put on them? I'm from the University of Montana, and I'm working with the National Park Service. Did you see the decal on my truck?"

"So?"

"So, you aren't allowed to kill animals here. They're protected. We've collared them, and we're studying them."

The man clears his throat, looks at the boy and at the squirrel.

I cup the little Columbian in my hand. There's only a small wound on his side. The bleeding is mostly internal.

They know I'm lying. They're within their rights. They can kill all the squirrels, snowshoe hares, coyotes, foxes, anything they want.

I can no longer look at either of these examples of *Homo sapiens*. Perhaps because I don't look at them, they remain silent.

I feel something wet, and I look down at the squirrel and see that he has released his bladder. The urine drips off my hand, through my fingers, onto the forest floor.

Rags the Digger died in 1927 when a man named Bill Caywood pumped two bullets into his heart. The old wolf had become a loner by then, having lost two mates. The first was shot as she ran beside him across the prairie. The second burned to death in her den along with her five pups. The smell of kerosene was strong outside the den, and it lingered for many days.

Cornelius Devny Morain couldn't know about the kerosene, but he could imagine that it was so. There's no electricity in his cabin. He uses a kerosene lantern when he writes.

I'd read the story the day the hermit gave it to me, and since then it had never been far from my mind. It didn't matter that the details had been altered, shaped and reshaped in the retellings; the story haunted me.

Now Andy sits by the fire in the lodge, manuscript in hand, the lamp pulled close. I'm curled on the couch beside him, content that he's finally here. The room is bathed in warmth and flickering light.

Dinner is finished, the dishes draining in the rack. The bottle of wine he brought is sitting on the coffee table in front of us. Outside a hard rain is falling.

"The hermit wrote this?" Andy asks.

"He said he heard the story from several different sources. He wanted to write it down so it wouldn't be lost."

Andy settles back into the chair and begins to read.

"You can't help but feel ashamed," I tell him, "after you've read it. "

He doesn't answer.

"It makes you look at things differently."

Again, no answer.

I get up from the couch and wander over to the windows. Through the rain-streaked glass I gaze out at the Bitterroot Mountains, thinking this may be the last time I will see them in this light.

"I thought about being a wildlife photographer when I first took this job," I say, loud enough for Andy to hear, but soft enough for him to ignore if he wants.

"Now I don't think so. Photographers only observe. Not that that isn't important. It just doesn't seem like what I should be doing with my life."

The rain is coming harder now. The mountains are blurring, disappearing into the horizon. I walk across the room and stand behind Andy. The handwriting is small, but there are parts of the manuscript I could almost recite from memory.

For a time Rags paired with a young white wolf, until she ate a ball of beef tallow laced with strychnine. She began frothing at the mouth. Her pace slowed and her legs stiffened. She tumbled and lay writhing in the Colorado dust, and her breath came in tortured gasps. She half rose, vomited strings of slobber, dropped and lay panting until her breathing slowed and then became imperceptible.

Rags watched her, but from a distance. No doubt he knew of the sickness that caused wolves to go mad.

The she-wolf gave a final shudder and lay still. Rags approached. He stood over her for a time, as if expecting her to rise and continue on their hunt. When she did not, and it seemed that she would never rise again, he moved on. Darkness fell, and the wolf climbed to the top of a high ridge and howled. His cry carried to distant places, and it went on for a long time. When it was done he left that mountainous place and set off alone. He would not mate again.

The rain pounds on the roof of the lodge. I wander around the room, approach the bookcase beneath the staircase, scan the titles. There are books on Wyatt and Virgil Earp, a dozen Zane Greys, Willa Cather's *My Antonia*, works by McMurtry, Steinbeck, Michener, and Thoreau. During the long winter nights I'd read most of them.

I pick up a book containing excerpts from the journals Thoreau kept for many years. The book falls open to a page I bookmarked several weeks ago. Andy is still engrossed in the story. I look at the entry I wanted to share with him:

> *When I consider that the nobler animals have been exterminated here, —the cougar, panther, lynx, wolverine, wolf, bear, moose, deer, the beaver, the turkey, etc.,—I cannot but feel as if I live in a tamed, and, as it were, emasculated country.*

I think back to the time when we first noticed there were no male squirrels in grid number four. I close the book, put it back on the shelf, but the words haunt me. "… (we) live in a tamed and … emasculated country." I glance at Andy, then back at the mountains.

Rags the Digger earned his name because of his raggedy coat and his uncanny ability to ruin trap lines. He could dig up the double-jawed, steel traps without springing them. To the ranchers and hunters who laid the traps it seemed as if he was taunting them. But this was a wolf who had long observed his tormentors. He had learned their ways, and he knew how to avoid their killing devices.

Then Bill Caywood, hired by the U.S. Government to rid the west of wolves, came for him. The bounty hunter tracked the wolf for many months, studying the prints he left behind, learning his habits, checking his scat, listening for howls. When he thought he was close, he chose a spot near a watering hole to lay his traps. He was careful to leave no trace of human scent.

Rags the Digger approached that night. Even in near darkness, the trap was obvious. One of the steel jaws was barely covered with dirt. Rags began to dig the earth from around the trap. When he'd completely uncovered it, he backed off, into the jaws of a second trap Caywood had hidden in the weeds.

The steel jaws closed on his leg and the wolf yelped in pain. He thrashed, and the three-pronged drag line attached to the trap snagged on a sapling. The line tightened. The sapling bent, but it held.

The wolf tried to bite through the steel jaws that held him. In his frenzy to escape, he stepped on the third trap Caywood had laid for him. Now two of his legs were caught.

Caywood, camped some distance away, heard the ruckus. He mounted his horse and rode to the spot.

The wolf no doubt felt the footfalls of the horse. He grew still.

The man approached the clearing, reined in his horse and dismounted. He took a Colt 45 from his saddlebag. He raised the gun, aimed, and squeezed the trigger.

The hammer made a clicking sound as it hit the bullet. Misfire.

Rags, watching the man's face, began moving toward the man. At great cost he dragged the two traps, the chains, the uprooted sapling, a rotted log that had snagged the second dragline.

Bill Caywood sighted along the barrel of his gun and squeezed again.

Again, the clicking sound. "God Almighty," Caywood muttered. He felt fear rise from his gut up into his throat.

The wolf came closer, his head raised toward the man.

He's going to attack, thought Caywood. Two legs caught, dragging a mountain of brush, and he means to attack me.

From the throat of the wolf came a sound. A whine. Caywood backed up, into the horse that should have run off by then, but had not.

He raised the gun a third time. This time it did not misfire.

The wolf was knocked back by the impact. He whimpered. Then he began to move forward again, reclaiming lost ground.

Caywood fired again.

The bullet hit the wolf squarely in the chest, and the chest spewed blood. Incredibly, the wolf still moved forward. When his nose was inches from the tip of Caywood's boot, he went down.

"I swear," Caywood said later, "He acted like he wanted me to help him get the traps off him. Even after I shot him. The way he kept coming at me, after I'd shot him twice, hit him square in the chest with the second shot, and still he kept coming. It was like he thought I'd help him."

It is said that Caywood knelt down and stroked the pelt of the old wolf he'd hunted for so many months, and that he regretted what he'd done.

Andy lays the manuscript aside and rises from his seat. "Quite a story," he says. He picks up his wine glass, walks to the window. "There was a campaign to exterminate all the wolves from the Great Plains back in the 1920s. The government hired professional hunters to kill them. Caywood must have been one of them. And Rags one of the renegade wolves." He twirls the wine glass in his fingers, looking down into the depths of the Cabernet. "It couldn't happen now," he says. "We know so much more about wildlife management and ecology and predator-prey relationships. The wolves in Yellowstone are thriving." He doesn't mention the ones who stray outside the park.

"Will the lynx reintroduction project go forward?" I ask, joining him by the window.

He sighs. "A lot will depend on the research."

"And on the ranchers."

"Yes. The ranchers."

"The rain has stopped," I tell him.

"In the morning we'll load up the rest of the bunnies, take them up to the grids, and release them."

"Did you know I named one of them Thoreau? He always had this quizzical look about him, as if he were trying to figure things out."

"And he preferred the company of animals to people? Like Thoreau?"

"That, too."

"Is he still here?"

"No, he's gone." Thoreau died a week after I moved the cages, but I don't tell Andy that. Already necropsied, his contribution to science noted, Thoreau is now a number who will one day appear on a chart that is part of a Master's thesis.

"Will you come back to Missoula with me?" Andy asks. "As soon as I'm finished writing up the results, I'll be starting a new project. I'll need an assistant."

"I've been thinking I might apply to veterinary school," I tell him. "I have all this money in my checking account. Over $16,000. Stuck out here in this wilderness, there's been no place to spend it. It's enough to get me started." I pause, then go on. "I think I might like to help that wolf. Rags the Digger. I could learn how to release those double-jawed steel traps Caywood laid for him. I could fix his legs. Then, when he was all better, I'd set him free. He could roam all over the West."

Andy looks at me quizzically, then throws his head back and laughs. Still laughing, he takes me in his arms. "Kylie," he says, nuzzling my neck.

"Will you wait for me? Give me some time to try to figure this out? Decide if vet school is the right thing for me?"

He's silent for a time. Then I feel his head incline toward me. "I'll wait," he says, and there's a softness in his voice I've only rarely heard before.

We stand by the window, the Bitterroot Mountains close, but covered in darkness.

THE EXTERN

It's two in the morning and the light from the hallway is streaming into our room. I hear Stephanie groan.

"All externs out of bed. They want you down in admitting." It sounds like one of the Green Card Mexicans who works the night shift here at Bryant Equine Hospital.

Stephanie sits up and I think she's about to throw a shoe, but the Mexican has pulled the door partway closed. He's safe on the other side.

"There's another colicky horse coming in," he yells. We hear his footsteps retreating down the hall.

There's more groaning and some choice expletives. Then three sets of extern feet hit the floor: Stephanie, Kim, and me, Kylie Wheeler, vet students from Colorado State, Cornell, and Texas A&M, in that order. We pull on yesterday's dirty jeans and shirts and head for the admitting area. Examination, blood work, evaluation; this is the protocol we've learned in the six weeks we've been here. When we're finished, we stand around and wait for the attending vet to decide what to do so we can please, please go back to bed.

Javiero, surgical resident from Madrid, Spain, is in charge. Banished from the daytime practice, he's been on night duty for the past week. Stephanie says he deserves it, but what does she know. She's a first-year student, and she thinks her looks will get her anything she wants. We've all seen the way she ogles Dr. Rocco. Kim dislikes her as much as I do, and it has nothing to do with her stylish blonde hair and Celine Dion figure. Sometimes I think she has no idea of the seriousness of this profession.

Two hours later we crawl back into our bunks, smelling of medicine, horse, sweat, frayed nerves, and exhaustion. It takes that long to examine, probe, test, analyze, and reach a decision. The mare will be okay 'til morning, Javiero has decided. We'll re-evaluate then.

I've seen horses biting at their sides with pain. Eyes wild with pain. Pawing the ground, drenched in sweat, cuts and scrapes all over their bodies from rolling.

Back to bed, and I pray they don't bring in any more emergencies.

But they do. Out there in the green Kentucky pastures is another sick horse that can't wait until morning. At least her owner thinks so, though why the owner didn't think that during the day is a profound mystery to all of us.

They call Dr. Rocco on this one. It must be an important client. We scrub in and watch the surgery, all three of us externs. Dr. Rocco is brilliant.

The horse dies on the table. We go back to bed, grab what sleep we can. I lie on top of my blanket on the upper bunk in this room we call home. I don't bother to undress.

I just kick off my boots and push them over the edge. I'm too tired to care if they land on Kim's bed beneath me. She won't care, either. She's nearly as dead as that horse over in surgery.

I wonder if the horse would have died if Javiero had been doing the anesthesiology instead of that sleepy tech Rocco called in. It's not Javiero's specialty, but he's at least as good as Dr. Sutherland, the new anesthesiologist they just hired. Why didn't Rocco call Sutherland, I wonder. Maybe the job description said there would be no night work. Maybe she wrote a contract for herself with a provision that they had to let her get her beauty sleep.

Anesthesia is such a tricky thing on a horse. There are so many things you have to watch. When you see something the slightest bit off, you have to react fast, and there's such a small margin for error. Javiero says he picked it up just observing, but I think he must have been paying close attention when he was in vet school.

One of the Mexicans will have wheeled the dead horse out of the surgical suite by now. He'll have taken her down to the building by the road and covered her with a tarp. The rendering truck will pick her up in the morning. A hefty bill will soon be on its way to the owner, who didn't notice there was anything wrong with the horse until the darkest hour of the night.

It's hard to go back to sleep when you know you have to be up again in an hour. It doesn't seem worthwhile. You know you might feel worse than if you never went back to bed at all.

The blinds are closed, the curtains pulled, but there's something different about the darkness beyond the windows. The sky is lightening, ever so subtly. I wish there was a way I could stretch this hour into two or three or ten. How will I ever make it to the end of the summer? It's only the middle of July, and already I'm so sleep deprived, I walk around in a fog most of the time. Maybe that's the point: they're trying to teach us to practice vet medicine in our sleep. They want the procedures to become like second nature to us.

I lie there waiting for the alarm to go off, thinking about the first colic that came in and the one that died. I wonder if the decisions we make in the night are the same as what we make in the daytime. Maybe we should revisit those decisions in the morning because they were made when it was dark and we were afraid. That's the real reason the owners load up their sick horses and bring them to the hospital. They're afraid, and the darkness magnifies their fears. That, plus the fact that the clinics they normally use aren't open. We're 24/7 here at Bryant.

Javiero is in the stall with the mare from last night when I get to the barn at 7 am. He glances at me but doesn't say anything. Maybe he doesn't even see me, he's that absorbed. I watch while he checks her heart rate and rhythm, respiration, temperature, gut sounds, digital pulses.

I like working with Javiero. He lets me do procedures the other vets are reluctant to entrust to an extern who's spent two years in the classroom but precious little time in a practice. When there are farm calls to be made, and it's Javiero's turn to take them, he'll ask me to come with him.

And if the owner doesn't mind, or is preoccupied, Javiero will let me draw blood or give injections or do whatever needs to be done.

I teach him things about vet medicine in America. We don't feel a horse, I tell him; we palpate. We don't listen for heart rhythms or gut sounds; we auscultate. He raises his eyebrows and repeats the words and phrases, as if he's never heard them before and wants to get the pronunciation just right.

When we're riding along those country roads, we talk about Texas and Spain and his wife back in Madrid and my boyfriend in Idaho. I tell him of my visit to the Rock of Gibraltar when I was in college and the caves of Altamira and the Hemingway books I've read.

Every Spaniard has a soft spot for the famous American novelist, he tells me. They've all read *Death in the Afternoon*. He talks about Madrid and his parents who were killed in a car bombing when he was three and the Basque rebellion in the North. His dream is to go back to Madrid and practice veterinary medicine as a board-certified equine surgeon.

Barns, even equine hospital barns, are pleasant in the early morning. The horses, impatient for their breakfast, look out over their half-doors and nicker at us. The coolness of the night lingers, and the world seems a simpler place.

The colic's name is written on the chalkboard beside her door: Sugar Mine. Someone must have loved her, to have given her a name like that. She probably has another name, some artful combination of sire and dam, registration papers tucked away in a bank vault in Louisville or Lexington.

"I think she's improved since she came in," Javiero says. "I'm hearing gut sounds, and her gums have pinked up. Still no poop, though." He slides the door shut and fixes the latch.

"You should try to get some sleep," I tell him.

"Walk with me," he says. "Over to the lab."

There's work to be done in the barn. But there are other externs. Stable hands. Vets and vet techs.

I walk with him. We talk about the mare and the other cases that have come in during the last few days. He asks if I'm planning to join an equine practice when I get my DVM.

He doesn't ask what I think he should do about Dr. Rocco, the vet who took him off day shift. Maybe he senses that I don't know what to tell him. Or maybe he's learned something about levels of professionalism, the caste system that exists, barriers that can't be bridged. He's a surgical resident from a country far away, and I'm a rising third-year vet student.

When I get back to the barn, I start on the morning TPRs: temperature, pulses, respiration, and orders from the night. The foundered horse looks good. We think he'll be okay. The horse with the partially-paralyzed face is happy to see me. He bobs his head up and down. He reminds me of a bay named Shiloh I used to ride when I was a teenager.

If I could order up a miracle for this horse, I would. He's been here for a week and he's shown no improvement whatsoever. I check the tube that delivers the medication to his eye. I spend more time than I should stroking his face, probing.

He needs that miracle. A bit more brain power would be nice, too, in case he's ever tempted to run flat out into a wooden fence post, which is what we think happened to him.

The cryptorchid yearling who eviscerated after his surgery is two days post-op, and he's doing well. But he has a long way to go. Who knows when his owner might decide to put his wallet back in his pocket.

The next stall is empty. I keep my head straight ahead when I walk past. I don't want to look. I don't like to remember.

Dr. Rocco was certain we could save the foal who was stabled there. The tendons in his back legs were so tight he could hardly stand. I bottle-fed him for ten days, and he fought hard to live. It surprised me, that he fought so hard.

Javiero used to come into the stall and watch while I fed the foal. It was a slow process, and Javiero would sit in the straw and tell me stories about Spain while I held the bottle. He often talked about the Andalusian horse farm where he grew up. The farm was owned by his uncle, his father's brother, who had taken him in when his parents were killed.

Maybe Javiero knew I was learning a hard lesson there in that stall with the baby horse: you have to steel yourself against some of the things that happen in vet medicine. You need to find a balance between caring and letting go. I let go long before the foal did. And then came the hardest part: having to watch while he struggled, and knowing it was hopeless.

Dr. Rocco blamed Javiero for the foal that died, but I couldn't see that it was Javiero's fault. It was no one's fault. What we did wasn't enough, and none of us can figure out why.

When I've finished one side of the barn, I keep going. Out
the back door, through the pasture, onto the road which
runs behind the hospital.

The mare in the lower paddock whinnies at me when I walk
past. I wish I'd brought a treat for her. Tonight I'll make sure
she's in the corner stall, and that she has fresh water and clean
bedding. She's to be euthanized tomorrow.

Her lungs and pleural cavity are filled with a yellow fluid
I got all over me the other day. Dr. Bryant told me to go shower
and throw my scrubs in the washer with plenty of disinfectant.
I did, but I didn't think it was anything I might catch.

It's a cloudy day; we'll have rain by afternoon. The rolling
hills and clusters of buildings look like a Grandma Moses
painting with green pastures, white fencing, houses shaded by
tall oaks, ponds on every farm. I walk along the road, an access
road off Route 24, thinking about the cases we've had, trying
to put the hard memories into some dark corner of my mind.

Dr. Rocco is in the barn bay when I get back. He's come down
from the main clinic building to check on the colicky mare
Javiero saw last night. She must be very special.

He motions for me to come into the stall. I'm yearning for
a cup of black coffee, but there's no time. I follow him into
the stall and take hold of the mare's halter.

Dr. Rocco is behind the mare, doing a palpation, and he
talks to her while he works. His voice is soft and it's quiet in
the stall. I stroke the mare's neck, then lay my head against
the side of her face. She smells of hay and warm summer.

I hear Dr. Rocco talking about the condition of her kidneys, her ovaries, and her small intestines. If he can't locate something, he tells the horse about it, then reassures her when he finds it. She's standing easy. It feels good standing there, resting my head against this horse. I drift off.

"Prepare her for surgery," Rocco says, and his voice booms through the barn. I wake up in a hurry, wondering how long I've been asleep. Thirty seconds? Five minutes? Rocco strips off his gloves, throws them into the trash barrel and heads toward the medicine room to check the schedule.

If he noticed that I nodded off, he doesn't mention it.

Javiero thought the mare had improved. She doesn't seem to be in as much pain as she was last night. But Dr. Rocco's decision is final. No one would ever question Dr. Rocco on a medical decision. He does most of the cutting in this place. When he says go to surgery, we go to surgery.

Still, I can't help but wonder if it wouldn't be better to wait. Even in the short time I've been here I've seen horses in a lot worse shape than this one. I run my hand down the mare's face, her shoulder, her belly, wondering who gave her that name. Sugar Mine.

When I get my degree, I'd like to practice the way Javiero does. He stands back, observes, and tries to figure out what's happening and how serious it is before he'll think of taking a horse to surgery. That's what he did last night when it was dark and I was so tired I could hardly stand. I kept wishing he'd hurry so we could all go back to bed, yet I knew he was doing the right thing.

Surgery is hard on a horse. You can cut on a cat or dog, and that's nothing compared to a horse. It's a tremendous assault on their systems.

Sometimes these things resolve on their own. That's what Javiero was hoping for—that the medication he administered and the procedures he did in the night would be effective, and by morning she'd have improved significantly.

Dr. Rocco has a different opinion. He says the mare has a twisted gut, and that she'll be dead in a few hours if we don't intervene.

"You're one lucky little mare," Dr. Rocco tells her as he walks back from the medicine room. "You're damn lucky they brought you here." Ears perked forward, she turns to watch him.

I close the half-door and stand by the main entrance, waiting for Dr. Rocco to leave. He brushes against me as he passes, touching my breasts.

He's done it before. There's nothing sexual about it. It's a territory thing. He wants me to back up, to give way. But I won't.

The first time it happened I stepped back and said I was sorry. For getting in his way. But I don't do that anymore. I stand my ground.

I watch him cross the grassy area between the barn and clinic. The clouds have dissipated and the sun has come out. It's bright on the horizon, and Dr. Rocco is walking directly into it. He's a large man, six foot four, tanned and muscular, a man who dominates wherever he goes. Once

I saw him crack a horse in the ribs so hard I thought for sure he'd broken one. He gets irritated with owners who pamper their horses. Yet he seems to like this little mare. Maybe it's because she's so submissive.

It worries me, that I'm so tired and so much of the day is still ahead of me. What if I get a medication wrong? If I make a mistake, Javiero will be the one to get in trouble. He's in his second year of residency here, but technically he's still a student, so he has to answer to the others: Dr. Rocco, Dr. Bryant, and Dr. Sutherland. That's the way things work around here.

My eyes burn. The mare smelled so nice. Sugar Mine. I hope she's okay. So many of the patients who come in here aren't. We're an equine hospital, so we don't get the easy cases. Owners call in the traveling vets for the simple things. What we get are the desperate cases. The hopeless ones. It seems like we have a barn full of horses that aren't likely to get any better.

The smell of coffee hits me when I open the back door of the main building. But there are only scorched dregs left in the bottom of the glass container. I begin to brew a fresh pot, then go into the office to check my email. Maybe there'll be a message from Andy. It's been so long since we've seen each other, I've nearly forgotten what he looks like.

Dr. Sutherland, the new anesthesiologist, comes into the office while I'm at the computer. She takes her mail from the cubby and flips through the letters and advertisements. Then she asks if I'd like to house-sit for her while she attends a conference in Chicago. "I'll be leaving Tuesday morning," she says. "I have a menagerie of animals out at my place that need taken care of. You could spend the night. There's lots of room."

Does that mean I'd be off call? That I could sleep through the night? "What if they needed me here? For emergencies?"

She shrugs. "You could always drive over if they were short-handed. My house is just a few miles away," she says.

She has two horses, two dogs, and a cat, she tells me. One of the dogs is old and blind. He's a favorite; she's had him since vet school. I'll need to take him for a walk in the morning and again at night, she says. The horses will have to be exercised. I'm to put them in the barn if we get one of those afternoon thunderstorms.

"We had two horses come in last night," I tell her. "Both colics." What I'm thinking is that I should throw my arms around her, I'm so grateful.

"I'll be glad to speak to Dr. Bryant, if you'd like. I'm sure he won't mind."

"How long will you be gone?" I ask.

"Why don't you come over tonight," she says, and she's sifting through her mail as she talks. "I could fix supper for us." She drops a handful into the trash.

Something in her tone worries me. But she's the doctor. She can order me to do anything she wants. And if I don't do what she asks, she can report me to Dr. Bryant and I can be on the road tomorrow, bad report on its way to Texas A&M. This girl doesn't fit in; she has a bad attitude. You ask her to do something and she gives you an argument.

Still, there's a yin and yang to everything. I have a dilapidated Honda Accord sitting out in the parking lot behind the hospital. The gas tank is half full and the tires are inflated. I can quit anytime I want.

Vet schools like their students to get experience in places like this, yet they're protective at the same time. My pharmacology professor warned me about the Bryant Equine Hospital. "Dr. Rocco and Dr. Bryant are enormously talented men," he said, "but they have big egos. They might be hard to get along with."

Dr. Bryant is famous for his work in the field of artificial insemination and animal surrogacy. Thanks to his groundbreaking research, scientists hope to one day use in vitro fertilizations and embryo transfers to repopulate species that are near extinction. Dr. Rocco has published numerous papers in scientific journals on new equine surgical techniques that improve patient outcomes.

"I'd like for you to get to know old Kyzer," Dr. Sutherland says. "That's my dog's name. Kyzer. He's almost totally blind, and he snaps at everyone." She's standing close behind me. "I'd want to make sure you get along with him."

"Maybe I could drive over to your house this afternoon and meet him."

Dr. Sutherland glances at her watch, shakes her head. "I can't leave until late today," she says.

At least 40 spam emails have accumulated in my account in just three days. I click them one after another: Internet Jokes, Vacation Giveaways, Supercharge your Sex Life, Refinance your Mortgage, Viagra online. There's no message from Andy.

"Hotmail is the worst," I tell Dr. Sutherland, and I send the junk mail to the trash bin.

"You should block the ones you don't want," she says. She leans over me, gazing at the screen.

I smell her perfume. I feel her hand, resting lightly on my shoulder, caressing me. I wish there was an email from Andy. But he hasn't written me in two weeks. I guess he's as busy as I am.

I pull my hair elastic out and let my hair fall over my shoulders. I put my hair back into the scrunchie. I get up from the computer and pour myself a cup of coffee. The idea of an undisturbed night of sleep sounds like heaven. Three nights in a bed in a room all by myself is more than I can imagine.

"Come over around six," she says. "It'll still be light outside, and I can show you around." She writes her address on a yellow sticky and hands it to me.

Maybe I can talk Kim or Stephanie into coming with me. They can sleep on the couch, or in the spare bedroom, if Dr. Sutherland has one. There would still be one extern at the hospital.

At lunchtime I grab a Nature Valley bar out of the fridge and take my Honda on a trial run to Dr. Sutherland's house. Dark clouds are moving in from the west. Before I've gone half a mile enormous drops of rain are pounding against the windshield.

Dr. Sutherland's farm is back a long narrow road that twists and turns, following fence lines to avoid crossing the lush green pastures. The barn is close to the road, the house hidden in a grove of ancient oak trees. The rain has darkened the barn, turning the gray weathered boards to black.

The barn doors are painted red. Double sliding doors, painted the reddest of red. So is the roof. I can hear the raindrops splattering on the tin. Hitting so hard it sounds like hail.

Javiero is sitting in the medicine room studying lab reports when I get back.

"Why aren't you sleeping?" I ask him.

He glances up at me, then back at the report. "It's hard to sleep during the day," he says. "I see the colic is scheduled for surgery."

I nod. "Dr. Rocco thinks she has a twisted gut."

He gets up and goes out to her stall. I hear him slide open the door. He's there for a long time. When he comes back, the look on his face is enigmatic. He drops into the chair again. "We make so many mistakes, sometimes I wish we could start all over again. Wipe the slate clean and start out fresh."

"Is this a mistake? Surgery on this horse?" I ask.

"What does it matter what I think? The decision has been made. Rocco's gonna cut."

I look at him, and I see how his eyes are shiny. Like all Spaniards, he's not very tall. But he has dark curly hair and perfect ivory skin, and he's so easy to look at. Who wouldn't want to sit across a table from him in a restaurant, candles, wine, sparkling silverware and china? Who wouldn't want to travel through life with him?

"It doesn't always turn out bad," I tell him. "We've had our share of successes. What about Dr. Bryant's horse?" Dr. Bryant brought his mare in to foal a week ago. There's nothing wrong with her, no need for her to be here, but we had an extra stall, and when you own the place, why not take advantage?

"What about the twin that came in the other day?" I continue. The two babies had come in together, without the mother. One died the first night. Kidney failure. We'd given him fluids and started him on Lasix, but we couldn't get them working. The other twin has problems, but he has a good chance.

Javiero looks at me. "What about that miniature down on the end?" he asks. "Kissimmee?"

I have to laugh. Kissimmee is a miniature stallion. Some farmer in Florida needs donor sperm, and he's been chosen.

"We can let the Mexicans take care of him," I answer. "They've been threatening to give him a dose of pink juice when we aren't looking." Pink juice. Pentobarbital. What we use to euthanize. What we'll use tomorrow on the mare down in the lower paddock, the one with the yellow gunk in her thorax.

This miniature is the meanest pony I've ever seen. He turns his back end to anyone who goes into his stall, getting himself in kicking position. We've seen more than one stable hand come flying through the door. They'll sit on the floor and nurse their bruises and curse the miniature until they can get up and limp away.

"It wasn't your fault, Javiero," I tell him. "The foal that died, the donkey. Neither of them was your fault. That's just the way Dr. Rocco is. When things go bad, he has to find someone to blame."

"I wish I'd never agreed to stay another year. If I'd applied somewhere else, I'd be finished by now."

"I can talk to my professors when I get back to Texas. There might be a spot for you there." He looks at me, and for a moment there's a flicker of hope in his eyes. Then he looks back at the stack of reports on the desk.

We both know he has to stay at the Bryant Hospital. He has to live through this, wrest whatever experience from it he can, no matter how hard it is. There is no other choice.

The donkey haunts him. She haunts all of us.

Javiero is one of the best vets I've ever seen. Yet I understand what he's feeling. He's under contract for another year, and if he doesn't finish, he'll never be certified. That's his dream, to be board certified so he can go back to Spain and practice there.

And if things don't get better between Javiero and Dr. Rocco, I don't know what might happen. How can he learn to be a surgeon if he's never allowed to observe surgeries? How can Rocco do this to him?

Rocco holds Javiero's future in his hands, and he knows it. And so does Javiero.

"What do you think I should do?" he asks, and he shouldn't be asking, and we both know it. But he is, and I have to answer him.

I take a deep breath. Dr. Rocco is testing you, I could tell him. He's making it as difficult for you as he possibly can. If you give up, he'll think he did the profession a favor, that you didn't belong.

But I don't know if he will understand, and I don't even know if it's true, what I'm thinking. Maybe Dr. Rocco just doesn't like him.

Javiero looks so discouraged, so beaten. It hurts, to see him so helpless, so lost. I can't tell him what I think he should do. Because I don't know.

"Rocco might be right about this mare," I tell him. "Who knows? We won't know for certain 'til he goes in. Maybe it's just that your styles are different. Try to get some sleep," I say to him. Knowing it's not enough, not what I want to say, not what he wants to hear. I wish I could touch him, touch his hands, his face. I wish I could wipe away the frown that creases his forehead.

It didn't start with the foal that died. It began with the donkey that came in a few weeks before.

"That's a dead donkey," Dr. Bryant said. We don't see much of Dr. Bryant. He has heart trouble, and he's not around much. Mostly he stays in his million-dollar mansion on the hill behind the hospital. When you're smart enough to build a practice that counts among its clients some of the richest families in Kentucky, you can afford places like that.

"I think I can save her," Dr. Rocco said.

"No way," said Dr. Bryant.

Rocco, who is taller than Dr. Bryant, tilted his head back to scan the upper shelf of the medicine cabinet. "Clean her up, pump her full of antibiotics—I think she has a chance."

Dr. Bryant looked irritated. He was already mad at the owners for letting the donkey get in such terrible shape. He'd tried to convince them to let him put the animal down, but they refused. Now here was Dr. Rocco, his hotshot employee, disagreeing with him, siding with the owners against him.

"I really think I can save her," Dr. Rocco repeated. He was standing behind the donkey, surveying the damage.

Something in his tone was just too much for Dr. Bryant. "You think so? You think you can bring her back? Okay, then let's get busy." He grabbed the most expensive antibiotic off the shelf and began to prepare an injection. "We'll just see what you can do," and he jabbed the needle into the donkey's backside.

The thing is, the owners of that poor donkey were as maggoty with guilt as was the animal. In my two years in Texas, in my whole life, I'd never seen an animal as bad off as that donkey. She'd given birth out in the pasture. Coyotes had eaten her baby, then they'd started on her.

"The owners didn't even know she was pregnant," Dr. Bryant said. "'The jack was in the other field. He couldn't have got at her.' That's what they told me. How do they think she got pregnant? What did he do, jump over the fence and then jump back again when he was done? 'We never saw a baby,' they said. 'She couldn't have been pregnant.'"

But she was. That was clear to anyone who bothered to look. Now she wasn't. And she never would be again. The owners hadn't checked on the donkey for weeks, maybe months. Now here they were, wanting Dr. Bryant to put her through more misery, just so they could assuage their guilt.

Dr. Bryant had no choice. The client rules. But he's a sharp old man. The higher the bill, the less guilt the owners will ultimately feel. Thus the antibiotic, which we hardly ever use and may not have been the drug of choice. I made a mental note to ask my professors when I returned to school in the fall.

I looked over at Javiero, to see what he thought of the antibiotic, but his head was down and I couldn't see his face.

So began ten days of hell.

Most of the care of the donkey fell on us externs, though the Mexicans did their share. They were always willing to help if Kim or I needed them. Someone had to pick up the slack for Stephanie, who seemed always on her cell phone with either her husband or her lawyer. She was getting a divorce, and her husband was desperate to stop it. He called 20 times a day.

For a while, things went well with the donkey. In just a few days we'd gotten rid of the maggots and cleaned her up. She looked a lot better. Several times a day I went into her stall and got her up. If I had time, I'd take her out for a stroll. Once I put her in a temporary pen out in the grass, so she could feel the sunshine.

She never wanted to stand for very long, and that worried me. Then, when she should have begun making real progress, she started losing ground. There was no reason that I could think of. She just seemed to give up. I talked to Javiero about it, and we went over her chart. He said he'd talk to Dr. Rocco or Dr. Bryant about her.

It seemed like Dr. Rocco was hardly ever around during that time. Maybe he was ashamed to be using his veterinary skills to save a donkey, when he's an equine surgeon of such wide renown.

She gave up, I think now. She just gave up. She'd been through so much, that now she didn't want to live any longer. One day I went into her stall, and she was down. I couldn't get her up. I tried everything I knew; I begged, I pleaded, I tried to lift her. I even prayed. Nothing worked.

I got angry. "Get up," I yelled at her. "Get up." I was so frustrated, I didn't know what to do. She wouldn't move. No matter what I did, she wouldn't respond. We were doing all we could, and she just wasn't responding. Why wouldn't she get up? Why wasn't she getting better?

I was so tired. I took my tray of meds back to the treatment room and went outside. I leaned against the fence, trying to calm myself.

When I went back to her stall, I noticed that her urine was bloody. I wrote it down on the chart, and I wrote a lot of other things. Who was supposed to be in charge of this animal? Was anyone checking on her? Did anyone care? Should we change antibiotics? I wrote stuff you aren't supposed to write in a chart. Then I went looking for Javiero.

He was nowhere around. Out on a farm call, the receptionist told me.

When I got back to the stall ten minutes later, the donkey was dead. I told one of the Mexicans to call Dr. Rocco, and then I sat down in the straw next to her and cried. You can't take care of an animal day after day, have it end like that, and not have your heart break.

Dr. Rocco came flying into the barn, arms swinging, heels clicking. "Why didn't someone call me? Where is Javiero? Why hasn't he been checking on this animal?" He was furious.

I got up and walked out of the barn and went to my room. I crawled up on the top bunk and pulled the covers over me.

Kim came into the room sometime later. It was dark outside, and I wondered how long I'd been asleep.

"Javiero is banished from the day shift," Kim said. "Dr. Rocco says he can't stand to look at him. He doesn't ever want to see Javiero again."

I lay on my bunk, trying to absorb what she'd said. How could Rocco do that? He was Javiero's mentor. Javiero had come from Madrid to study under Rocco and Bryant. Rocco had talked Javiero into staying for the second year, and now it seemed that Rocco was trying to run him off, wash him out of the practice and the profession.

Javiero's world was tumbling down. His dream was dying. Without a recommendation from Dr. Bryant and Dr. Rocco, he would never be board certified.

It occurred to me that I wasn't so much physically tired as I was tired to death of inflated egos, personality clashes, turf fights, and territory markers. All these things were getting in the way of good veterinary medicine.

I didn't believe for a minute that the donkey was Javiero's fault, but if he really was banished from the daytime practice, I wouldn't be seeing him so much anymore. I wouldn't have to look at him and see defeat in his eyes. Defeat and fear. I wondered: would that be a comfort to me, or another heartbreak?

I thought about the donkey and how nothing we did for her really helped. In the end it was all for nothing. All we did was prolong her suffering.

I scrub in for the colic surgery that afternoon. Already anesthetized in the adjoining cell, the sleeping horse has been hoisted onto a table and wheeled into the surgery room. She lies on her back, draped, head and belly exposed, a block between her teeth. Dr. Sutherland is at her head, Dr. Rocco beside her.

The room is full of vets, externs, and techs. Everyone on staff seems to be here. Except for Javiero. He's in his quarters.

There's a window between the hallway and the surgery. The owners of the mare are standing there. I don't think I'll ever get used to that, seeing the owners at the window watching everything that happens.

The window is large enough so two people can stand side by side. They can even lean their elbows on the windowsill, if they want. Just like at a car wash.

I look over at them. Large, distinguished-looking man, graying at the temples. Blonde woman, tanned, wispy thin. Maybe she's his daughter. But probably not. Wife. Second or third.

There are advantages to letting the owners see what's happening to their animals. When they get the bill, they're more likely to sit down and write a check if they've actually witnessed what we've done. Watching an equine surgery can be impressive. And if something goes wrong, the teamwork and the drama in this place can be awe-inspiring.

If there's a difficult decision to be made, the owners are right there. I've seen vets invite them into the surgery while the horse is still under. Dr. Rocco is at his best in situations like that. He knows how to handle the owners, how to push them toward a "correct" decision.

He talks to the mare while he's working. And it's mesmerizing. Like there's no one else in the room but the two of them. He tells her she's beautiful, so young and pretty. Such fine lines. He's certain he can fix what's wrong inside her. If she'll just hold on, bear with the pain, he's sorry about that, but it'll all be worth it. She can trust him. She'll come through this just fine.

Suddenly there's a pounding rain on the roof, crashing thunder, and flickering lights. It all seems to happen at once. Stephanie, standing close to Rocco, looks up at the ceiling. Has the building been struck? The auxiliary power kicks in, the generator hums, stops, starts again.

Dr. Sutherland makes a noise that sounds like panic. I see her glance from her instruments to Dr. Rocco and back to the instruments. The room goes quiet while she adjusts the flow of meds, checks IV connections, catheters, the endotracheal tube. Then she waits, watching the draped horse. I think she's actually holding her breath.

She nods to Rocco. The crisis has passed. Surgery resumes. But now it drags, Dr. Rocco sweating through his clothing, Dr. Sutherland watching her monitors, adjusting the anesthesia, checking, adjusting again. There's a sense of dread in the room. As if Death has entered and is waiting to claim his prize.

Was it only this morning that I laid my head against this mare's neck and fell asleep? I wish Javiero were here. I want this horse to be okay. I would trust her in Javiero's hands.

Dr. Rocco looks up from his work and blinks, perhaps realizing we are there. He'd forgotten that in his concentration. "She's one lucky horse," he tells us. "Lucky to have owners like she does." He begins to describe what he's encountering deep inside the horse, what anomalies, what we should look for when we do this, what it should feel like.

Then he goes back to addressing the horse. His voice softens, and he repeats some of the things he said to her in the stall this morning.

When the surgery is finished, he goes into the observation room to talk to the owners.

Owner. The woman has gone outside. Dr. Rocco motions for the man to follow him down the hallway that leads to the reception room. I go back to watching the tech close the incision.

The job of the extern in surgery is to watch. Hand instruments, if the doctor calls for them. Do whatever we're told to do.

I'm watching the mare, noting her steady breathing, wondering how long before she's out of danger. I step closer to look at the line of sutures that run down the midline of her belly. It hits me then, sudden and hard. It's all I can do to keep quiet.

I never saw Rocco untwist the twisted gut. I saw him up to his elbows in intestine, but I never saw him untwist anything. If he found a displaced colon, I never saw him put it back into place. If he removed a section of intestine and reconnected the ends, I didn't see it.

Maybe there was no twisted gut. Maybe he couldn't find it. Or maybe it had resolved, like Javiero thought it might.

I wish Javiero were here. I wish I could talk to him. I wish the summer would end and I could go back to school.

Dr. Sutherland is out in the hallway. "Six-thirty?"

"I'm sorry," I tell her. "I can't come for dinner. My friend Andy is flying into Louisville, and I promised to meet him at the airport."

She looks surprised.

"I didn't know he was coming. He left a message on my cell phone. He's giving a paper at a conference in Washington. It's about his research on snowshoe hares. He's a biologist."

"Oh," she says, "well …"

"He's only here for a few hours. A layover, between planes. He won't get in 'til seven-thirty. Could I come by your house earlier? Meet the dog, and you could show me what you want me to do?"

"Fine," she says. "Come by anytime." She turns toward the door.

"Is five-thirty okay?"

"Sure. See you then."

I watch her walk out the clinic door, and I feel awful. Did I misjudge her? Was there an easier way to handle this?

I'm still standing in the hallway when I hear Dr. Rocco come in the front door. There's a muffled conversation, then Rocco's voice: "Go practice on that mare down in the lower paddock," he says. "We're gonna euthanize her tomorrow, anyway."

The mare with the fluid in her lungs? Practice what, I wonder?

Stephanie comes into the hallway, walks through the storage room. I watch her go into our bedroom and close the door.

I follow her into the room. "What about the mare down in the lower paddock?"

"I'm gonna insert a nasogastric tube," she says. "I've never done it before. Dr. Rocco said I could practice on her."

"Practice on her?"

"Yes. Practice on her."

"Well, you can't."

"Dr. Rocco says I can." She strips off her scrubs, pulls on shorts and a tank top. "Why would you care, anyway?" she asks. "Javiero lets you do all kinds of procedures." She walks out of the room.

Because I do. Because I made a promise to that mare. We have to put her down, and I accept that, but how we do it is important. How she spends her last hours matters to me.

Maybe I'll be the one who washes out. All this time I've been worried about Javiero, but maybe it's me who can't make the grade, gets too emotional, and can't stand to make the hard decisions. I go out the back door to the parking lot.

I'm sitting in my car, wondering what it would feel like to start the engine and drive away, when Dr. Sutherland comes by. I roll down my window. "I'm sorry, Dr. Sutherland. About dinner. I'll take good care of your animals, I promise."

"You sound upset. Was it the surgery?"

"No. Well, maybe. I guess that's part of it. Do you think she'll be okay?"

"Probably. I thought we were gonna lose her there for a few minutes, but she came through it. She's young. I think she'll make it, if she doesn't get an infection. That's the big worry now."

I'd like to ask if she thought the surgery was necessary. Did she see something I missed? Should Dr. Rocco have waited, like Javiero thought?

But I don't ask these things. Dr. Rocco is a colleague, and I can't ask her to betray him. Besides, it's better not to know.

"It's good that your friend is coming," Dr. Sutherland says. "You look like you could use some time off." She starts toward her pickup, changes her mind and comes back. "Kylie, there's not a vet anywhere who hasn't made a mistake, and won't continue to make them, no matter how hard we try. All we can do is our best, and realize the good we do far outweighs the bad. Understand?"

I nod.

"If you let the mistakes get to you, you might as well give up." She stands by my rusty old Honda, looking down at me. "My dog Kyzer? It's my fault he's blind. The machine I was using when I was in vet school malfunctioned. He went without oxygen for too long, and I didn't call for assistance when I should have. For a while he was deaf, too, but he got his hearing back. Most of it, anyway. But not his vision."

She gazes off toward the horizon. "I do what I can for him," she says. "I owe him that. But I don't give up." She looks back at me. "And you can't either. You're too smart for that. You have to go on."

Suddenly I don't give a damn about her sexual orientation. She's offered me a respite from this place, and I'm grateful. And ashamed that I judged her so harshly.

The blue tarp is gone when I go out to get the mare. The moon hasn't come up yet, but I can see the outline of the three-sided shed by the road, the dark shadow of the mare in the pasture. I climb over the fence and walk toward the sound of her breathing; it's ragged and labored. She stands with her head lowered, her nose nearly touching the ground. She's not grazing, only standing there trying to breathe.

There's no nicker of recognition when she sees me, no ears perked forward, no search for treats. I stroke her neck, slip the halter over her head, and begin to lead her toward the gate where Javiero is waiting. She walks slowly.

There isn't much I can do for her except what I promised: clean straw, fresh water, hay and a bit of grain if she wants it. And I can groom her; brush her face with a soft-bristled brush, curry her shoulders and flanks.

Javiero opens the gate, closes it behind us. We walk side by side toward the barn, the horse trailing along behind. One of the Mexicans has readied a stall for her. Rocco is standing at the upper end of the barn, filling up the doorway with his bulk. Even from the distance, I can see that he's watching us.

"He's probably come to check on the surgery he did this afternoon," I tell Javiero. She's a valuable horse; Dr. Rocco's treatment of her can only be called aggressive.

"It could be a long night," Javiero says.

I know what he means. If the outcome isn't good, Javiero will be held responsible. Yet the surgery Rocco did was so massively invasive, the horse so violated by what's been done, you can almost count on infection.

We enter the barn: Javiero, the doomed horse, and me. I don't look at Dr. Rocco as we walk past him, but I lift my chin and straighten my back.

"Why are you bringing that horse into the barn?" Rocco asks.

"I'm gonna try to make her a little more comfortable," Javiero says.

"She's being euthanized in the morning," Rocco says. "The owners signed the papers this afternoon."

"I know. Kylie told me."

"So what's the point? Take her back out to the pasture. We're not about to waste a clean stall on her."

"I'm sorry, Dr. Rocco. I can't do that."

I take a deep breath and keep walking down the barn bay, trying to focus on the rhythmic sound of our footsteps.

"I told one of the externs she could practice on her in the morning."

"There won't be any externs practicing on this horse," Javiero says.

We stop walking. Except for the labored breathing of the sick mare, the barn is abnormally quiet.

"What did you say?"

"There won't be anyone practicing on this horse."

"Why not?" Rocco's voice is sneering, ugly.

"Because that's not the kind of medicine I've been taught to practice. It's not the way I was trained. There are other horses your extern can practice on. But not this one."

"What possible difference could it make?"

"She's suffered enough," Javiero says. "No more."

The two men look at each other, and Rocco's face is dark with anger. "I think you've forgotten what your position is here at this hospital. I could have you fired for this. I can see to it that you never get another position in this country. You'll never get your certification, in surgery or anything else. You'll be on the next plane back to Spain."

"Put the mare in the stall down on the end," Javiero tells me, then turns back to Rocco. "Dr. Bryant's mare foaled about an hour ago," he says, and his voice is so soft I can barely hear him. "Your extern can go practice on her. She can practice on the colt, if she wants. But not this horse. I'll resign before I'll let you or anyone else do that to this mare."

The three stable hands who were working in different parts of the barn have each found a reason to draw near to where we stand.

"If you'd like, we can go talk this over with Dr. Bryant," Javiero says. "He was here a while ago. He came in to see his foal and to check on the surgery you did this afternoon. The owners are friends of his. Kylie, take the mare down to the stall."

"Or better yet," Javiero continues, still looking at Dr. Rocco, "let your student practice on Kissimmee. The miniature stallion down there on the end. He's due for a tube worming, anyway. The stable hands will be happy to help her."

Rocco stares at Javiero, then throws down the lead rope he's been holding. He wheels as neatly as any dressage horse ever wheeled in a ring. His boots clomp against the concrete floor as he walks out of the barn.

My hands are shaking and my insides churning, but I lead the mare down the bay and into the newly prepared stall. Javiero takes off her halter, places his stethoscope on her belly. I grab a soft brush from the rack and begin to groom her. It feels good to have something to do.

They don't castrate their stallions in Spain. I remember Javiero telling me that one day when we were on a farm call outside Lexington. He was describing the Andalusian stallions of his youth, how they looked in the ring when they were performing. "They're all fire and spin," he said. He talked about the classical dressage the horses perform, similar to that of the Portuguese Lipizzaners, only better, and his pride in his country and all things Spanish shown in his eyes.

Someday I'd like to see the things he's seen. I'd like to travel to the farm where he grew up. I want to see the decorated stallions performing their dance, spin and fire, fire and spin.

We geld all but a few of our stallions in the U.S.

In all of Spain, there are only two equine surgeons who trained in the U.S. When Javiero finishes this residency at the Bryant Equine Hospital or wherever he goes, he'll be the third. I have no doubt of it. Somehow, he'll persevere.

Javiero looks at me over the back of the mare. "I've been thinking, Kylie. If we could drain off some of that fluid, I think she'd feel a lot better."

I blink back tears.

He reaches across and brushes my cheek, and his touch is so light I'm not certain he even touched me at all. "Would you like to assist?" he asks.

I nod. Of course I would. I'd like nothing better.

FROM FARROW TO FORK

"Pull over, Dan," Dr. Hincheon says. "Let someone else take the wheel for a while. Dan, can you hear me? Are you all right?"

"I hear you. I'm all right."

Something in his voice sets off an alarm inside my head. I sit up and look over the seat at my two professors.

"No, you're not," Dr. Hincheon says. "You need to pull over. Come on, Dan, there's a place up on the right. Stop the car and let someone else drive. You need a break."

"I'm fine. Just fine."

But clearly he is not. His speech is lazy, slurred. He veers to the center of the road, corrects, goes off into the gravel, corrects again. Mark Shipley, riding next to me, awakens with a start. "Did we hit something?" he asks.

"No," I tell him. "Put your seat belt on." I untangle the belt and push it toward him.

Mark looks back at the cloud of dust we've stirred up, buckles the belt around him. I hear him take a deep breath, then exhale.

There are four of us in the Ford Explorer, two veterinarian clinicians in front and two fourth-year vet students in back. We're on our way to the Women's Maximum Security Prison in Hentonville, Texas. We've been on the road since five-thirty this morning. It'll be another hour before we get there.

Dr. Dan Oastin is driving, Dr. Hincheon riding shotgun.

"No, Dan, you're sweating like crazy," Dr. Hincheon says. "You need to check your blood sugar. Come on, Dan."

Dan keeps driving. For a while I think he's slowing. Then he accelerates. He's gripping the steering wheel hard, like it's going to save him, if he can just hold on.

I look at the speedometer. Seventy. Seventy-five. Eighty. The road ahead of us is Texas straight, nothing on the landscape but stunted trees and scrub brush, very little traffic. Dr. Hincheon isn't likely to try to take the wheel away from him, not at this speed.

"Dr. Oastin, please pull over," I lean forward and put my hand on his shoulder. I can feel him trembling. "Let Dr. Hincheon drive for a while. Or one of us. Mark can drive, or I can take the wheel. You need something to eat. I have some juice in my lunch bag. You can have it. Please pull over. We need to check your blood sugar."

"Kylie?" He blinks, looks at me in the rear view mirror, blinks again. He seems confused, as if he's wondering why I'm here. He wipes a hand across his forehead, the back of his neck.

"Yes, Dr. Oastin, it's Kylie. Your speech is all garbled. You know what that means."

He sighs. "Hypo …," but he can't finish the word. He takes his foot off the accelerator, and the SUV begins to slow. Dr. Hincheon helps him steer to the side of the road.

Somehow, I've gotten through to him. The feminine touch, maybe, though I hate to admit it.

Mark looks over at me. I think he's grateful, which must be a new feeling for him. Like many male vet students, Mark doesn't believe women ought to be going into a profession that historically belonged to men. Nor should they be siphoning off resources that could have gone elsewhere. For three years Mark and I have been in competition for the annual scholarship given by the Graduating Class of 1950. For three years running I've won it.

The recipient for this year's scholarship hasn't been announced yet, but last week I had my picture taken for the fourth time. They plan to use it on the cover of the annual fundraising brochure they send to their classmates. The photographer promised to send me prints, but I already know what the picture will show: one white-coated female vet student surrounded by 25 old men.

The veterinarians who graduated in 1950 are, without exception, white-haired old men. In their eighties now, they use walkers, canes, wheelchairs. More than a few put their teeth in a glass of water beside their bed at night. I doubt any of them use Crest Whitestrips.

Still, it's fun, having my picture taken with them. If they have reservations about giving money to a girl, they try not to show it. The world is changing. They're scientists, and they know they need to change with it. So they give me the scholarship money, and it helps me stay in school.

I know the challenges ahead of me. I stand five foot three. Not tall enough to be a large animal vet, they tell me. I weigh 110 pounds. Not strong enough, they say. I have brown hair streaked blonde by the Texas sun. Blue eyes. Not tough enough to make the hard decisions. Too sentimental. Too emotional.

I wonder if what they say is true. My plan is to keep inching forward, keep doing the best I can. The challenge this year will be to put into practice everything I've learned in the last three. That's what these rotations are all about. I've done well with the academic part, but this is different. Now I'm working with live animals, and I'm responsible for what happens to them.

A semi blows past us, sounding his air horn. Our exit from the interstate has not been smooth.

When the SUV comes to a stop, Dr. Hincheon hurries around to the driver's side. Dan tries to step out of the vehicle, but his legs are rubbery, his body trembling. Dr. Hincheon grabs him around the waist, motions for Mark to help. The three of them begin walking toward a stand of trees. Dan's blue shirt is dark with sweat. He can hardly move his legs.

Somehow they get him away from the road, over to the trees. They sit him down in the shade.

I'm busy opening the juice I brought for my lunch, stripping the wrapping off the Nutri-Grain bar. I glance over at Dan, sitting propped against a tree, and I'm afraid for him. My dad is diabetic. I know how bad it can be.

I rummage in the center compartment between the front seats, find Dan's glucose meter, grab it and run toward them.

It occurs to me I'll have to eat prison food when we get to Hentonville. There'll be no time to run out to the nearest town for lunch. They might put McDonald's in college food courts, but not in maximum security prisons.

I shove the straw into the box of apple juice and hand it to Dr. Oastin. "Drink it, Dan. It'll make you feel better." I unzip the pouch with his diabetic supplies, grab a lancet and prick his finger. His hand is so cold it's hard to get the blood I need for the test. I squeeze his finger and see the pain register on his face, but I get a drop of blood on the test strip. Within a few seconds the One Touch Ultra comes up with the reading: blood sugar 35.

I hand him the Nutri-Grain. "Eat this, Dan. It's a cereal bar. Apple Cinnamon. And drink the juice. You need sugar. Come on, Dan. Take a bite."

What am I doing calling him Dan? This man is forty years older than me. He's my professor and the lead clinician on this prison rotation.

But I know why. "Dan" might register in his sugar-starved brain, where "Dr. Oastin" might not. They teach us useful things like that in vet school. When you're working with a sick dog or cat, and you call him by his name, you're doing it for the animal but also for the owner, who's probably standing there assessing you, wondering if you have the skills to do what you're doing, and are you worth the money you're going to charge.

Why didn't I bring a banana? But the juice is good.

He sips from the box, takes a few bites of the cereal bar, and slowly he comes back. The paleness leaves his cheeks; his eyes begin to focus. He's okay.

"Sorry about that," he says, chewing on the bar. "I guess I put you all in danger, didn't I?"

"No, we had everything under control," Dr. Hincheon says. "As soon as you're feeling better, we'll head on down the road. They've got a barnyard full of livestock waiting for us."

"I can usually tell when my blood sugar is low," Dan says, and he sounds like the old Dr. Oastin. "But sometimes I have no idea. I thought I was all right."

"You're fine, Dr. Oastin," I tell him. "You just needed a little sugar. It helps the brain work better."

"I guess I turned my insulin pump too high this morning." He tries to smile, but can't quite bring it off.

"Did you have any breakfast?"

"Maybe I forgot," he says.

Ten minutes later we pile into the SUV and head down the interstate, Dr. Hincheon driving this time, Dan beside him in the passenger seat. I settle back in the cushy upholstery, hoping to grab an hour of sleep before we get to the prison.

I close my eyes and think about the day ahead of us. Horses to be wormed, a herd of Brangus cattle to be vaccinated, who knows what else. I've been to half a dozen prisons since this rotation began, and I'm still amazed at the variety of animals they have at these farms: horses, cattle, dogs, cats, an occasional bird. I hope they don't have pigs at this prison. I've had my share of pigs.

The truth is, this is not my favorite rotation. I've been through anesthesia, small animal surgery, neurology, and public health. What we're dealing with now are primarily food animals. Our job is to treat animals that are born and raised for the consumption of Texas prisoners. The *Farrow to Fork Program,* they call it.

If we help the animals, that's only accidental. Our real goal is to make sure the humans who come in contact with them don't get sick. That's a problem for me.

And yet, if we'd had the brucellosis vaccine when my grandfather was alive, he might not have suffered like he did. He contracted the human version of the disease, undulant fever, when he was in his mid-fifties. For years he was plagued with undulating fevers, blinding headaches, chills, and night sweats. At times the disease seemed to go into remission. Then it would come roaring back.

My dad once told me of seeing his father sitting in the kitchen of the old farmhouse, blinds closed, rivulets of sweat running down his face, the headache so bad he could only hold his head in his hands and rock back and forth. Sometimes his tears would mix with the sweat, my father said, and the old man would moan softly until the pain medication finally took effect, and he could sleep.

He'd had the disease for several years when the family doctor drove out to the farm one afternoon, bringing with him an experimental drug. It was a brand new drug that had never been used before. There would be no charge because its effects were unknown, but surely worth a try considering the severity of the disease. The doctor insisted, though, that my grandfather sign a paper holding the pharmaceutical company free from any liability.

What I think they probably gave him was tetracycline, and it might have worked. If he'd stayed on it long enough. If they'd given him a large enough dosage. It was all so new back then.

I wonder if he'd be proud if he could see me now, six months from graduation, riding in this great black bruiser of a car filled with medicines, vaccines, needles, tubes, restraints, ropes, cages, the car sailing across the flat Texas countryside. Six months away from earning my DVM. Thirty years too late to help my grandfather.

Most Texas highways are straight and smooth, and the Explorer eats up the concrete. It seems as if we're hardly back on the road when I see the prison looming ahead: a cluster of buildings low on the horizon looking like a medieval walled city, flat-roofed buildings of all shapes and sizes, smokestacks rising into the air, watchtowers and floodlights placed at measured intervals around the chain-link perimeter. The surrounding countryside is a checkerboard of cultivated fields and pastures. In a distant field I can make out guards on horseback, prisoners with hoes. The guards wear khaki, the prisoners white.

Dr. Hincheon slows the vehicle as we approach the main gates of the prison. He waves to the armed guard, and we pass through. The Texas A&M decal on the side of the Explorer is all the identification we need. They've been expecting us.

As we drive into the prison complex, I notice loops of razor wire above the chain-link fence. It surprises me that they'd need razor wire at a women's prison, but it shouldn't. This is a maximum security prison. More than a few Texas women have made national headlines for both the originality and the brutality of their crimes.

I crack open my window to smell the air.

"What's the matter, Kylie? Afraid we'll have to bleed some more pigs?"

I look at Mark and groan. "Some of them didn't have jugular veins, I swear they didn't."

"Retractable jugulars?" he laughs.

"You didn't do much better," I tell him. I close the window and sink back in my seat.

It was true. Mark had as hard a time as I did. We both began to wonder if Oastin and Hincheon had brought us along to do the grunt work, the work they didn't want to do anymore. We were in our twenties, they in their sixties. Creaky joints, slow reflexes, a certain jaded quality; they'd done it all so many times.

As part of our prison rotation, our professors had taken us to the Walker County Maximum Security Prison for Men two days before. The work crew at the prison had slaughtered a number of animals the previous week, and one of the boars had tested positive for porcine brucellosis. That brought a call to our vet school. All the animals at the prison had to be tested. Texas is trying hard to eradicate the disease so they can get some of that nice USDA money the federal government is handing out to the other 49 states.

I felt sorry for the pigs. Great dumb animals at the mercy of ravenous, flesh-eating mankind. Poor lactating sows, having to feed their babies through a mesh wire. Each piglet grown to adulthood represented so many prison meals. They had to be protected from mothers who might inadvertently roll on them.

Despite the wire barrier, I pulled three dead babies out of the pens. Holding those still pink bodies, I began to consider again whether or not I should become a vegetarian. It's a debate I have with myself about once a month. Someday I'll decide.

By the time we finished, I hated the pigs. Hated every single one of them. To get blood from the jugular of a 400-pound boar is an accomplishment like no other. They scream so loud you think your eardrums are about to burst. They don't stop. It's absolutely non-stop, their screaming, and you think you'll surely go crazy if you don't get away from them. Why didn't Hincheon and Oastin tell us to bring earplugs?

I'm always amazed at the tricks we learn in vet school, the special ways of handling an animal that make it possible for us to work on an enraged bull that weighs thousands of pounds. Or on a squirming pig that weighs several hundred.

A group of prisoners pin the victim between two gates. Then about ten of them hold down every body part they can hang on to, the pig screaming the whole time.

The poor vet student has to lean down under that massive animal, find the vein in the neck, and fill a vial with blood. I'd stab this way and that among those thick rolls of skin, trying to hit the jugular. My legs went numb from having to squat so low, and for most of the afternoon I felt like a complete incompetent.

When the last pig was released, I was splattered with blood, my hair was rank, my clothes soaked with sweat and other foul things. Twenty boars, forty sows, the sows weighing only slightly less than the boars. Trying to get blood from their jugulars was like fishing in a lake with a needle. It was nearly impossible.

They served ham sandwiches for lunch that day in the prison dining room. I ate one. It was sweet revenge.

Today I'd packed my lunch. Nutri-Grain breakfast bar, apple juice, cheese cubes and wheat crackers. All I have left is the cheese. Dan ate the crackers after he finished the cereal bar.

"Relax, darlin," Mark says. "It's a women's prison. They don't have any pigs here. Just horses and cows. Maybe some bloodhounds."

He knows I hate that, calling me darlin'. I look out the window.

"The wardens probably figure women prisoners are too squeamish for things like castrating pigs and butchering."

Mark is Texas born and bred. It's the only excuse I can come up with for remarks like that.

I pull my baseball cap down over my eyes. Dr. Hincheon weaves his way among the buildings, heading for the equine barn.

The inmate they assign me is a woman named Charlie Caswell. I look at her, and I'd like to ask her many things, but it's against the rules. No personal inquiries. We must conduct ourselves at all times like the professionals we are.

Wonder all you like, but do your job and don't ask questions, we've been told.

Her hair is dusty brown, long and unkempt. Like her body. She can't be more than thirty-five, but she's 50 pounds over-weight and already sagging: face, posture, demeanor.

She stares at me, as if she'd like to ask a hundred questions. Here's what I'd like to ask her: What did you do to get in here? Is Charlie your real name? Do you have children? Are there things in your life you would do differently, if given the chance? Do you have a boyfriend? A husband? Do you look at me and wonder why our lives are so different?

Charlie evidently knows the rules as well as I do. She does whatever I ask, she answers when I speak to her, but she volunteers nothing.

We start with the kennel horses, horses specially trained to run with the bloodhounds in case of a prison escape. Charlie takes a halter from the tack room and heads for the corral while I lay out the supplies and begin to soak the nasogastric tube in warm water. She grabs onto the mane of one of the horses, slips the halter over his head, and leads him into the bay. Together we back him into a corner, and I apply the twitch. Insert the tube into the nostril, the pharynx, rub the neck to encourage him to swallow, check and double check to be certain the tube is in the esophagus and not the trachea—we don't need any dead horses today—then on into the stomach. Smell for stomach contents, put in the medication, then water to wash it down. Remove the naso tube, take off the twitch, and send the horse into the opposite paddock.

When the kennel horses are done, we start on the line horses, and the rhythm we've established makes the work go quickly. An easy banter springs up between us, but it is a banter that does not stray into personal areas.

She begins to offer bits of information about the horses. She knows them well. This one lost a foal back in the spring, that one had a baby that sold for a thousand dollars, the big gray out in the pasture is the best cutting horse she's ever seen.

I ask about the horses we saw patrolling the perimeter of the fields where inmates were working earlier in the day. Shouldn't they be brought in for worming?

"They're mostly personal favorites of the guards," Charlie says, and she gazes out toward the fields. "They're on a different schedule."

She's standing very still, and I look at her profile; from that angle she is strikingly beautiful. I imagine she's thinking about freedom, yearning to be away from this place, yearning to be anywhere but here.

How long does she have to serve, I wonder. Is she here for years? For life?

The work with the horses is finished by lunchtime. There was only one nosebleed, the horse spewing out an enormous amount of blood, but it stopped after a while. Charlie has seen it happen during previous wormings, and she didn't panic. Horses can lose a lot of blood, and it doesn't seem to bother them.

I head for the main building to meet up with my co-workers. We'll do the vaccinations and any other work they have for us in the afternoon. With luck we'll make it home in time for dinner.

The chalkboard at the entrance of the building shows a drawing of a plate of food, a frosty glass of liquid. The menu is written below: Macaroni and Cheese, Mashed Sweet Potatoes, Cornbread, Sweetened Iced Tea.

We grab utensils, napkins, and slide our trays along the railing in front of the steam tables. Dr. Oastin is ahead of me in the line. The servers behind the tables load up his plate. He heads out into the dining room. I get my food and follow.

I watch to see if he turns up the insulin pump attached to his belt. He'll need to, with high-carb food like this.

The temperature has soared while we were in the dining hall. We walk out into the central courtyard area of the prison, and it feels as if we've entered the vestibule of hell. The sun is directly overhead and spread over an inordinate amount of sky. The air is deadly calm.

Mark, Dan, and Dr. Hincheon resettle their hats on their heads and start for the western section of the compound where the cattle are corralled. I twist my hair into a knot, pile it inside my baseball cap, and follow. Dr. Hincheon detours to the horse barn to bring the SUV around.

The sun is burning my face, my arms, the back of my neck. I yearn to be back in the mess hall with its rotating fans, sipping the cold tea with slivers of ice floating on top, feeling the glass sweating onto the raw wooden tables.

I'd even settle for the shade of the barn where Mark and I worked with the horses earlier in the day.

A quarter mile away, I see dust rising from the milling cattle. I can smell dung and smoke and raw fear in the air. There's another smell, too: the odor of burnt hair and singed flesh. It's such a distinctive, acrid smell, it could be nothing else. They're branding the young stock.

The clear afternoon is punctuated with the unearthly bellowing of the cattle, many brought in from the range for the first time. They're terrified by the noise, the fire, the unfamiliarity of it all.

My stomach churns. What's an Alabama girl doing in a place like this? Do they really still need to brand cattle? Isn't there some other way, some modern method?

I glance at Mark, remembering what he'd said about women prisoners. These are women separating the cattle, hotshotting them, running them into chutes, tending the fire, wielding the branding irons. These are women who dressed this morning in their prison whites, whites that are now stained with the muck and gore of the jobs they do every day of their imprisonment.

I hear footsteps behind me. It's Charlie, hurrying to catch up. I stop to wait for her.

"You gonna be my assistant this afternoon?" I ask.

"No, I haven't been assigned."

She matches her pace to mine. "I wanted to ask you this morning. There's a dog in the tack room," she says. "One of the horses stepped on him. I wonder if you could look at him. When you're finished with the cattle."

I hesitate. "Is he yours?"

"I've been taking care of him."

"When did it happen?"

"Four days ago." She wipes a dirty sleeve across her forehead. "I think he needs to be put down," she says.

I take a deep breath of the fetid air. "Maybe I could ask one of my professors."

"If you could just look at him," she says.

"I'll need to get permission," I tell her. "I'm not really a vet, you know. Not yet."

"He's in the tack room," she says. "Underneath the stairs. I've been feeding him, and he ate at first, but then he stopped. Now he won't even drink water."

Four days. Enough time for infection to set in. Internal injuries. Broken ribs, maybe. "I'll look at him. As soon as I can. Otherwise I'll ask Dr. Oastin. He owes me."

"I think he's hurt bad," she says.

"I'll do something. I promise."

Hincheon drives past, dusting us with another layer of dirt we don't need. He parks the SUV near the closest corral.

There must be a hundred cows penned in the several enclosures. They mill about, paw the ground, lock horns with each other, run from the women who hold the prods and wield the lashes.

If the courtyard is the vestibule of hell, now we've moved several steps closer to the main gates.

The women don't look like women. Prisoners and guards alike, they are a sinewy mess of hard-muscled bodies and sun-leathered skin. No guns here, the keepers and their charges blend in a way you don't see in the men's prisons. They are all caught in a system that long ago ground away any soft edges they might have had. In this place they can no longer act like women. It may be hard to act like a human being.

But watching Charlie melt into the melee, it strikes me that she is still very much a woman.

It's been four days since the dog was trampled, she said. Four days hidden under the stairs in the tack room.

Our work for the afternoon is clean and simple. We are to vaccinate and tag the heifers. Dr. Oastin and Dr. Hincheon take their places on opposite sides of a special pen. At a signal from one of them, a prisoner stationed inside the corral opens a gate. A cow sees the opening. She runs toward it. The gate slams shut behind her. As does the one in front. She's trapped.

Dr. Oastin jams the needle containing the vaccine into her shoulder. Dr. Hincheon calls out a number and staples a tag in her ear. A prisoner opens the front gate and the cow runs off, kicking up her back legs at this unexpected freedom. Safe in the new corral, she turns to look, her eyes wild, her tail twitching, her breathing fast and shallow.

It's a sweet operation. All carefully planned and executed. The two clinicians vaccinate and tag a dozen cows in the next fifteen minutes. There's only one casualty. An out-of-control Brangus hits the front gate so hard we hear her neck snap.

"You don't see that happen very often," Hincheon remarks. He motions for a group of prisoners to drag her out of the enclosure.

Mark and I take over, and the work resumes. We're fourth-year vet students, after all. We've vaccinated hundreds of Texas cows. We can handle this.

Oastin watches from the sidelines for a few minutes, then drifts off. He's promised to look at one of the prison bloodhounds kenneled behind the cattle barn. Hincheon, finished with his examination of the dead Brangus, goes off to find a shady spot where he can return his cell phone calls.

Mark sits on the top rail on one side of the chute, me on the other, and we alternate. He vaccinates, I tag. I vaccinate, he tags.

We're nearly finished when we run out of vaccine. Neither of our professors is anywhere in sight.

How hard can it be to reconstitute the drug? I watched Dr. Oastin do it earlier in the day. There are still 20 or 30 cows waiting in the holding pens. I climb down from the fence and go to the SUV, open the chest that holds the vaccine.

Mark is leaning against the side of the pen. The heifer in the chute is bellowing, twisting, banging against the sides. The sun is broiling hot.

I remove one of the special needles that's sharp on both ends. Push one end into the water, pull water into the needle. Push the other end into the bottle of vaccine. Inject the water into the powder.

The dry vaccine explodes out of the bottle. A cloud of live vaccine swirls around me. It covers my hands, my face. Live brucellosis vaccine. Airborne.

"Mark?" I call out, and instantly regret it. If I don't breathe, maybe I can keep the bacteria out of my lungs.

Better to keep my eyes closed, too. But then I see my grandfather sitting in his chair in the kitchen of the old farmhouse, holding his head in his hands, rocking back and forth with the pain. I think about the undulating fevers so typical of the disease, the headaches that left him whimpering, the torrents of sweat that rolled off him.

What will Dr. Oastin say when he finds out what's happened? What made me think I could do it on my own? Why was I so arrogant?

I watched him mix the vaccine with the water just a few hours ago, and I thought I was doing it exactly the way he did it. But I missed something. I did something wrong.

I reach up to touch my face. I can feel the granules of dust and the mist from the needle. I open my eyes and look toward the enclosure. "Mark?" I call again, and my voice is breathy from lack of oxygen.

"Oh my God, Kylie, what happened?" He's there, beside me. "What happened, Kylie?" he repeats, but he already knows, he saw it happen, saw the burst of vaccine. He grabs my arm, pulls me toward the nearest building. Then we're in a bathroom, and he turns on both faucets and dunks my hands under the stream.

"Get it off your skin as fast as you can, Kylie. Use lots of soap. You'd think they'd have a brush in here. Do you have any cuts? Open wounds?"

I soap my hands and arms, then hold them under the stream of water. "It exploded out of the bottle. I thought I was doing it like Oastin did. I don't know what went wrong."

When I've scrubbed my hands until they're red, he fills up the sink with water. "Now your face, Kylie. Scoop up the water and wash your face. Your hair, too. We should find you a shower."

He looks around.

Charlie is there. Standing by the door, watching. She comes forward. "I'll take her," she says.

Numb with fear, dripping wet, my thoughts a jumble, I follow her out of the building.

The shower room is huge, large enough for a dozen women or more. Charlie turns on the water, comes to help me undress.

"No, you don't want to get it on you," I tell her. "Can you find me a garbage bag? Something to put my clothes in?"

The water is cold. I stand under the shower, waiting for it to warm. After a while I give up. I use the cake of soap—do the prisoners make this too, I wonder—to shampoo my hair and scrub my body until I'm certain nothing remains. The water seems colder than when I began.

I'm shivering by the time I've finished. Charlie is there, holding a towel for me, a change of clothes over her arm. Prison white, too big, but clothes. They'll get me back to College Station.

"Do you ever get to shower in warm water?" I ask, toweling my body to try to get warm.

She shakes her head. "No," she says, smiling ever so slightly at my naïveté.

Dr. Oastin is waiting outside the building. "What happened?" he asks, and his voice is stern.

I look at him, and I have no words.

"You're supposed to break the water vial in the vaccine," he says. "The vacuum causes the water to mix with the powder. What did you do wrong?"

"Shut up, Dr. Oastin," Mark says, so quietly I wonder if I heard correctly.

"I did break it," I tell Oastin, glancing at Mark. "But the vacuum had been compromised. I don't know how. The powder sprayed all over me."

"Any cuts? Do you have any cuts? Your hands? Your face?"

I hold out my hands. He takes them in his, sees the scraped knuckles, the cut on my wrist.

"I got that from a cow who threw her head up when I was tagging her. A few days ago, I think. I can't remember exactly."

"I doubt if you have anything to worry about," he says, releasing my hands, looking now at my face. "I dropped a needle one time and it stuck in my leg. I took tetracycline as a precaution."

He brushes my wet hair back from my face, glares at me. "This vaccine isn't nearly as bad as what we used to use," he says, turning my head from side to side.

I wish he'd quit talking. I've heard all this before. He's talked about it in class. I know all about undulant fever. More than I need to know.

"The RV 19, that was bad. If you vaccinated an animal with RV 19, she'd test positive for brucellosis for the rest of her life. But the stuff we use today, the RV 51, it's not nearly as bad.

"When we get back, I'll drive you over to the clinic for some tetracycline. Take it for a few weeks and you'll be fine." He puts an arm around my shoulders, and we begin walking toward the SUV.

I'm sitting in the front seat when I remember Charlie. "Dr. Oastin, would you go down to the horse barn and take a look at a dog down there? He's in the tack room. He was trampled by one of the horses a few days ago."

He hesitates, looks over at Dr. Hincheon. Our work here is done, we should get back. It'll be long past dark before we get home.

"It's not a bloodhound," I tell him. "Not a prison dog. Just a stray that wandered in. But he means something to Charlie. The woman who helped me this morning. Would you?"

"Come on, Mark," he says, tossing his head. "Give me a hand."

I watch them walk toward the horse barn, thinking that Dr. Oastin will never make it for his 50th year reunion picture.

I wonder if I will.

We head back toward College Station, Dr. Oastin driving once again. He likes the Explorer, likes the power of this great vehicle, the feeling of invincibility when he's at the wheel.

I sit in the front seat next to him, trying not to think about what happened.

The insignia on the dash reminds me it's a Ford Explorer. Edsel Ford, son of Henry Ford, died of undulant fever. He got it from drinking unpasteurized milk, it is theorized. Cattle were not widely tested for brucellosis back then, nor were they immunized.

I look over at Dr. Oastin, wondering if he knows this bit of history. If he did, he would likely incorporate it into his lectures. But I don't want to share it with him.

I wonder how I came to know it. Did my father tell me? I lay my head back against the seat and close my eyes.

Neither Dr. Oastin nor Mark said anything about the dog when they returned from the equine barn, so I didn't ask. I knew what their silence meant. I wasn't really expecting a happy ending. Not for Charlie, or for her dog.

I'll start the tetracycline in the morning. Five hundred milligrams every six hours. If it doesn't work, there are other drugs I can try. I'll be okay.

DOMINION

I KNOW IT'S TIME for me to move on when the farmer with no zipper in his pants runs his hand down the horse's withers and says he thinks he'll just wait and see if the horse might get better on his own.

The horse, upper lip curled, swings his head toward the offending hand, to bite or to knock it away. I see his muscles contract as he tries to distract himself from the pain.

I glance at Dr. Parker, equine veterinarian at Lancaster County Animal Clinic, wondering how she's going to handle this. She's been dreading the call; she's talked of nothing else since we left the clinic.

"He's much worse than he was last night," Dr. Parker tells Mr. Hostetler. "I don't hold out much hope for him."

The bearded man fidgets with the straps of his suspenders. Amish wives sew the clothing for their families. Buttons are too decorative, and thus not allowed. Zippers are too mechanical. Hooks and eyes must suffice. Suspenders do a nice job of keeping the pants from falling down.

"He isn't worth anything," Hostetler says, kicking a flake of hay into the feed trough. "I just keep him around for the kids to ride."

"He'll need something for the pain," she tells him. "A colic death can be pretty hard."

"I thank you," he says, "but we'll just see what happens." He slaps his hat against his leg. "The boys have been taking him for a walk around the pasture every few hours. But then he started rolling, and I was worried they might get hurt, so we penned him up."

Dr. Parker sighs. "I'm sorry, Mr. Hostetler. It's an awful way to die. And it isn't quick."

He runs his fingers around the brim of his hat. "Well," he says. "God's will be done."

I look hard at the man, bite my lower lip and say nothing.

"There's a surgery we can do," Dr. Parker says. "He's a young horse. Depending on what's causing the colic, it might be worthwhile."

"But the cost," Hostetler says.

She nods. "I know. Upwards of $5000. And no guarantees."

"I can buy three horses like him for that," he says.

"We can euthanize him, if you like."

Hostetler looks from Dr. Parker to me, clearly wanting a second opinion.

"It's an option," I offer, uneasy with the situation. Gillian Parker is the vet he's used to dealing with. I'm only riding with her for the day to get a feel for the practice, in case I decide to accept the job they're offering me. This is the first of three veterinarian practices I plan to visit over the next two days.

It's a buyer's market for new vets fresh out of school. My DVM degree is so new it's still in the tube. When the Journal of the American Veterinary Medical Association (AVMA) magazine comes in the mail addressed to Dr. Kylie Wheeler, it takes me a minute to realize that's me.

The classified ads in the back of the magazine show how many jobs there are out there, how many over-worked vets who are desperate to hire someone to help them in their clinics and practices.

My wedding ring is new, too, though the diamond is old. It once belonged to Andy's grandmother, who died ten years ago. Andy had the stone put in a new setting.

Hostetler looks away, and I sense his disappointment in my answer. He's gotten used to Gillian, but now here's another woman vet. Where are the men? A male veterinarian might see things differently.

Women in the Amish tradition are subject to their husbands. Maybe women in all traditions are subject to their husbands; I can only take this job if Andy can find a college or university in the area where he might want to work.

I stroke the horse's neck. "It would probably be best," I tell the farmer, "to put him down."

"I think I'll just wait," Hostetler says, turning back to Gillian. "He might come through it all right." He moves the hat he's holding round and round in his hands. The brim is perfectly straight, the edges sharp as honed steel.

Do the women make the hats as well, or are there hatters in the community, I wonder.

Gillian sighs. "I'll leave something with you for the pain," she says. "And I'll check on him later this afternoon."

"No, you needn't bother," he says. "We'll get by."

I solemnly swear to use my scientific knowledge and skill for … the relief of animal suffering … The words of the oath I swore a few short months ago come back to me.

But they have no import here in Lancaster County, Pennsylvania. This is something I'll have to get used to, if I'm to succeed in this profession. The horse belongs to this bearded Amish man, and his word is final. There's nothing for us to do but get in the truck and go on to the next call.

The three children who've been working in the garden below the house look up when we emerge from the barn. I'd seen them earlier: two boys and a girl, all dressed in shades of gray, the girl wearing braids beneath a white cap.

The boys lean on their hoes and watch as we climb into Gillian's truck, but the girl flings her rake aside and runs to her father, who is standing outside the milk house.

He holds out his arms to her, and she flies into his embrace.

We get into the truck, and Gillian pulls away. She does not look back.

"I'd have loaded that horse up with drugs," I tell her when we're safely away from the farm.

"He doesn't have the money to pay for them," she answers.

I look out at the impossible green of the fields, the brick houses, the red barns, the white fences. "What do you imagine he's going to tell that little girl? About the horse?"

"Whatever he tells her, she'll accept it. You heard what he said: 'God's will be done.' They see things like this as part of God's plan. Did you notice he paid me in cash?"

"They don't use banks?"

"No banks, no electricity, no motors. There are exceptions, of course, but they try to avoid contact with the outside world, as much as possible. They're known as 'The Plain People.'"

Plain People. People who read the Bible by candlelight each evening. People who believe they have dominion over animals.

I'd have given the drugs. Despite what Hostetler said. I'd have done it.

The horse will die. In excruciating pain.

Barns in Lancaster County smell of old milk. Most of the dairies have been closed for years, yet the scent lingers. The concrete floors are swept clean, the ceiling beams white-washed, the pens heaped with clean straw. Stanchions have been removed, milking parlors torn out, trenches filled in.

The milk houses are always cool, even on the hottest days. The aluminum coolers have been sold, the wash-up sinks dismantled, the tubes that connected the parlors to the milk houses removed. Suspended in time, the rooms wait for some new use, and they are cool in their waiting.

Gillian and I travel from one farm to another as she works through her calls, and she talks about the practice.

The herds of cattle are gone, she tells me, with only a few kept for the needs of the family. Like Mr. Hostetler, many of the farmers keep a few horses. They use them to plow the fields, pull wagons, carry the family to church. They keep them for pleasure, and out of sentimentality.

Many of the families have opened shops where they sell ice cream, hamburgers, fresh fruits and vegetables in summer, canned foods and homemade jellies in winter.

When the calls are finished, we stop at one of these shops before heading back to the clinic. We sit on cane-backed stools, and Gillian orders strawberry milkshakes from the teenaged girl who stands quietly behind the counter.

"Will you go back to Hostetler's place tonight?" I ask after the girl has gone into the back room. "To check on the horse?"

"No," she says. "He wouldn't approve." She sips her drink. "Maybe I'll go anyway. I could tell him I was driving by, just stopped to see how the horse was doing."

"Any chance he'll change his mind? Let you put the horse down?"

She shakes her head. "I doubt it," she says. She stirs her drink with the straw. "They aren't cruel people, Kylie. I'm sure he cares for the horse, and he doesn't want to hurt his family. But they live isolated lives, and they prefer it that way. They try to avoid anything that might break down the family unit. Cars, public schools outside their community …" She hesitates, and I see a smile steal across her face. "Hostetler couldn't call me if he wanted. He doesn't have a phone."

"No phone? How does he get in touch with you?"

"He comes in person, horse and buggy, or he sends word with a neighbor. They watch out for each other."

The girl returns, and our conversation ceases. I finish my drink and check my cell phone for the local time. My plane leaves in just over three hours. I have a long night ahead of me: flights from Philadelphia to Atlanta to Raleigh, where I pick up a rental car and drive to Fayetteville, North Carolina.

Lancaster County is not the place for me.

I want to go out into the world, not retreat from it. I want to live my life focused on the work I have chosen, not on the eternity that might come after. The last line of the Veterinarian's Oath, to *"accept as a lifelong obligation the continual improvement of my professional knowledge and competence,"* would not be possible here.

I think of the girl in the white apron, and I wonder if she will ever experience the miracles of technology, know the joy of learning, feel the thrill of pushing beyond the limits of knowledge. Will she ever have a cell phone, and will she marvel, as I once did, how a cell phone knows what time zone it's in as soon as you turn it on?

This is not where I belong. I won't ask Andy to check out nearby universities where he might get a job.

A gentle rain has begun to fall when we leave the ice cream shop, and it seems to fit my mood.

"I have to get to Atlanta tonight," I tell the clerk at the Delta counter in Philadelphia. "I have an interview in the morning."

"I'm sorry," she says. "Your plane is still in Chicago."

"Chicago?"

"All flights out of O'Hare have been grounded. There's a front moving through." She places the e-ticket I handed her back on the counter.

"Can you get me on another flight?"

"I'm sorry. The storm has everything backed up."

"But it's barely raining here. Surely there are planes coming from the Northeast: New York or Boston. I really need to get to Atlanta tonight."

"There are no availabilities." She looks down at her monitor, begins typing.

"Could you check other airlines?"

"I'm sorry, Miss. There are no availabilities. I'll book you out on the first plane in the morning."

"What am I supposed to do tonight?"

"You can take a shuttle to one of the local hotels. There's a phone with direct lines to the hotels downstairs opposite baggage. Take the escalator."

"I don't have money for a hotel."

"We don't give hotel vouchers for weather-related delays." She pushes the e-ticket closer to me. "There's a flight at 7:03 in the morning I can get you on."

I look at her name tag. Lucinda Denton. "Look, Miss Denton, I have to get out tonight. Otherwise I'll never make my connection. If I don't make my connection, I can't make the interview. This is my first job. I have to get to Atlanta tonight."

"I'm sorry," she says. "I can't control the weather. If you don't want me to book this flight for you, would you please step away from the counter? I have other customers waiting." She crumples some papers, throws them in the wastebasket, moves her stapler, straightens her pens, and begins typing again.

"Please, Miss Denton. Lucinda. This interview is really important to me."

She signals for the next passenger to come forward. A family of three begins to wrestle their bags toward the counter.

I don't move. I stand there, looking at her. "Can you at least refund the money I paid for the ticket? So I can go to another airline?"

The family stops, uncertain. I've kept my voice level, but they heard what I said.

"I'm not authorized to do that." She busies herself with the items on her work area, rearranging and straightening them again.

I wait. I keep looking at her.

She hooks her hair back behind her ears, then disappears through a door just beyond the luggage conveyor belt. She emerges a few minutes later with another airline official.

"I'll help you down here," the man says, signaling for me to follow him to the far end of the counter.

Ten minutes later I'm booked on a flight due to arrive within the hour from Bangor, Maine. I don't know if he found an empty seat or he bumped another passenger, and I don't ask. I tell him how grateful I am for his help.

The rain is heavy now; I can hear it drumming on the roof. The wind is blowing sheets of water against the windows. But it doesn't matter. With any luck at all, I'll get to Atlanta in time to make my connection. I need to get far away from the thought of what's happening in that barn back in Lancaster County.

I always have anxiety when I fly, and tonight, with everything that's happened, it's worse than ever. My hands are cold, just thinking about all the things that could still go wrong.

I remember that I have a few Diazepam in my purse. A half tab might just take the edge off my fears.

A third of the housewives in the fifties took Valium, the brand name for Diazepam. It helped them get through the day, they said. Many believed it kept them out of insane asylums.

We use it in vet medicine to treat problems of inappropriate elimination in felines. Of all the benzodiazepines available to us, Diazepam works the best. It's effective in 75 percent of cases, and it has fewer side effects than Buspirone, Amitriptyline, or Prozac. Occasionally it wrecks the liver, but that's a risk worth taking if the alternative is euthanasia. Which it often is.

In one of my final rotations in vet school I prescribed it for a cat who was peeing on her owner's Karastan rug. The husband wanted to put the cat down. I gave them a supply of Diazepam and told them to bring the cat back in a week. Maybe it saved her life. They didn't come back, so I never knew.

Just before I board the plane I break a pill in half, wash it down with water from the bottle I'm carrying in my shoulder bag. The dosage is small, only a milligram, but in no time at all I begin to feel warm and relaxed. Maybe I'll be able to nap on the flight down to Atlanta.

Twenty minutes out of Philadelphia the pilot apologizes for the bumpy ride. He tells us the storm is moving faster than predicted. The flight attendants should take their seats. He's been cleared to climb to 38,000 feet, and he hopes the air will be smoother there. He plans to take some evasive actions as well. We might be a few minutes late getting to Atlanta, but he'll try to make up some time when we're clear of the weather. Stay in your seats and keep your seat belts securely buckled, he says.

The plane shudders, creaks, and strains as we fly through the turbulent weather. Lightening fractures the sky off the right side of the plane. I pull down the shade, determined not to look out the window again.

I take the remaining half pill, close my eyes, and try to believe in God. Not the Amish God: that God might have plans for me that are different from mine. He might be angry that I disapproved of his good and faithful servant Hostetler, who is probably sitting in his living room at this moment, surrounded by his wife and children, reading from his Bible by the light of a candle.

I almost wish I were there … except I could never keep my mind on what he was reading. I'd want to be out in the barn, doing whatever I could for that poor horse.

After what seems like hours, we finally find some smooth air, and I feel safe enough to let my mind drift.

The perfect job for me would be in a mixed practice of both large and small animals. The facility would be clean and spacious and equipped with the latest technologies. The practice can't be so large that everything is specialized, or so small that I have to be on call sixty or seventy hours a week. Most importantly, it has to be a clinic that practices modern veterinary medicine.

There are certain things I look for when I visit a practice. I like to walk into the surgery and see how the surgeons are dressed. Are they gowned, or only gloved? So many vets don't bother with the gowns; they're too busy, and the risk of contamination is small. But the risk is there, I would argue.

Do they scrub up to their elbows, or just wash their hands? Are the surgical rooms big and roomy? Are the sinks large and plentiful? Do the vets monitor the patient when the surgery is over, or do they just glance inside the mouth to check the color of the gums, then go on to the next task?

Even on a simple spay I like to monitor everything. I leave the oxygen on for a few minutes after I shut off the anesthesia. What are the pain management protocols? Do they send small animals home with pain medication? Do they even have pain management protocols?

When I ask questions during an interview or a walk-through, I choose my words carefully. I know how people will judge me. They'll say I'm young and idealistic. When I've been practicing for a few years, I'll get over it.

I hope that isn't true.

There's another reason for turning down the job in Lancaster County. Inside the medicine cabinet at the clinic I saw a supply of FIP vaccine. Feline Infectious Peritonitis. Gillian said they don't use it, but if that's true, why haven't they thrown it out? Recent studies indicate it's a bad vaccine. By introducing healthy cats to the virus, it actually makes them more susceptible to the disease, which is 100 percent fatal.

Maybe the practices in Fayetteville will be different. There are four universities within driving distance, and Andy is confident he can find a position at one of them.

The Hostetler family with their candles and Bible, their house with no phone, and the bay horse seem many miles away and far back in time.

My flight to Raleigh has already left by the time I arrive in Atlanta. The airline officials couldn't be more accommodating. They book me on an Air France flight. Even in my semi-drugged state, I know Air France does not fly milk runs between Atlanta and Raleigh, nor does it operate twenty-passenger prop planes, but I don't question it. I board the plane, and in just over an hour we've landed. It feels good to be back in the South. I pick up my rental car and head for Fayetteville.

Driving down Bragg Boulevard, I think I must be in Vegas. Fayetteville is a city full of nightclubs and strip joints. It glistens with neon, and it vibrates with music and laughter. Fort Bragg, the major U.S. Army Installation, home of 50,000 soldiers, is just five miles to the west.

Two hours later, when I arrive at the Days Inn in the Cape Fear River Valley, I'm confronted with another woman behind another counter. This one is older and more tired than the Delta woman in Philadelphia. Her hair is too red, her makeup too heavy, lipstick too dark and too far outside the natural lines of her mouth. She lists the amenities in the room she's selected for me: coffeemaker, hairdryer, TV, iron and ironing board. She runs my credit card and slides the key across the counter.

A man approaches as I walk toward the lobby door. He says something to me, but I don't understand.

"Excuse me?"

He repeats the sentence, but it is lost on me.

"I'm sorry. Could you say that again?"

He does. But I can't make out a single word.

He's thirty something, wearing khaki pants and a blue shirt open at the throat. Too well-dressed to be homeless, I judge. Not retarded or dangerous, but he has a look of uncertainty on his face.

Is he a soldier on leave? Is he asking for directions? His words are totally indecipherable. I wonder if he's speaking some strange combination of low-country Carolina mixed with a generous helping of deep-fried Southern. But I was raised in Birmingham, Alabama, as deeply Southern as you can get, and I've never heard anything like it.

There's nothing to do but ignore him. Pulling my suitcase behind me, I open the door and step outside. The rain is heavy. Heat lightning flashes in the western sky. The headline in the local newspaper beckons me:

Pets Abandoned When Owners Deployed

Standing under the portico, I pick up a copy and scan the article:

> *… more and more military personnel being de-*
> *ployed overseas … network of support systems …*
> *domestic pets a largely forgotten casualty …*
> *few options for pet owners … shelter at Fort*
> *Bragg has a 90% kill rate for dogs, 95% for cats …*

I put the newspaper back in the rack. The man has followed me out of the lobby. He's standing just outside the door. Hugging the building to try to stay dry, I begin walking toward my room. He follows.

I turn to face him. "Listen, Sir, I can't understand what you're saying. But I want you to stop following me."

He answers, but again his words are incoherent. He's standing in the rain, making no attempt to shelter himself.

"Will you please stop following me? Would you just go away?" What does he think? That I'm going to invite him into my room?

The raindrops are splattering his shirt, turning the shoulders a dark blue. Rivulets of water run down his face. I wonder if he understands a word I've said.

I take a deep breath. "Do you speak English? Sir? Listen to me. I want you to stop following me. I want you to go away."

He half smiles.

"Stop following me," I shout at him. "Stop. Go away."

He holds out his hands to me, palms up. Does he want money? Or is he saying he's harmless, that he has no intention of hurting me?

I'm tired and angry, and I don't care what he wants. I wheel my suitcase around him, walk back to the lobby. I fling open the door, stomp inside. "Call 911," I tell the woman. "This man won't stop following me."

She looks up at me, blinks, opens her mouth to speak but says nothing.

I turn around. The man has entered the lobby. He stands quietly by the door, hands folded.

"Would you please call 911?" I ask again, my voice lower. "I can't understand a word he's saying, and he keeps following me."

She looks at the man, sizing him up with a practiced eye. "I'll give you another room," she says.

"I don't want another room. I want you to call the police."

"Listen, honey, we wouldn't want to get the police involved. I'll give you a room close to the office." She looks back at the man, squinting now. "He hasn't done anything, has he?"

What a moron she is. "He's following me," I shout at her. "He acts like he wants to get into my room. Call the police."

"I don't think that's necessary, Ms. Wheeler. Unless he's done something . . ." She taps her pencil on the edge of the counter, a Morse code of uncertainty. "I'll give you a new room and make sure you get there. I'll walk you to the door if you want."

I look at her, then at the man.

"I'll make sure he knows you're a guest," she says.

I stare at her. A guest? As opposed to what?

"I'll keep an eye on him," she says.

What are my chances of finding another motel at this time of night? Cape Fear River Valley: I should have been forewarned when I booked the room. Fayetteville. Fatalville. Fayettenam. A tough military town made famous by its frequency of spousal abuse, spousal killings. Summer of 2008, four Fort Bragg soldiers killed their wives in a span of six weeks. Two of the men later committed suicide.

"Is there a lock on the door?"

"Yes, there's a lock. The room is just a few doors down the walkway."

"What kind of lock?"

"Several. You'll be safe."

There are actually four locks: a push-button in the knob, a turn lock directly below the knob, a deadbolt above it, and a chain above that.

When the woman is gone, I close the door and engage all four. I tug the drapes closed, pull the table over to the door.

I pick up the phone, listen for the dial tone, touch zero. Six rings later the woman answers. "This is Kylie Wheeler in Room 106. Doctor Wheeler. I just wanted to make sure I could reach you."

"I'll be here until seven in the morning," she says.

I hang up and move the phone close to the bed.

I should call Andy. But what can I say to him? That I booked a room at the Days Inn for $40 a night, and a man I can't understand tried to follow me to my room? I can't tell him that. And if I did, what would he say? What could he do?

I'm shivering in my wet clothes, but I'm afraid to take a shower. What if he tries to break in?

The hotel phone is by my bed. There are four locks on my door. The clerk is only a short distance away. I can reach her anytime I want. I walk to the door, stand by it, and listen. There's no sound, just the rain and the occasional crash of thunder.

It's 12:30 at night. I've been up since five this morning. I pick up my cell phone and touch #2 for home. It rings five times, but Andy does not pick up. I imagine him asleep in our bed, the ceiling fan turning above him.

I unzip my suitcase, take out my cosmetic bag, robe, and nightgown. I'm in the shower when the lights go out. I stand under the water, waiting for them to come back on, or for the generator to kick in. All commercial establishments are required to have generators in case of power outages.

The lights flicker on, then go off again. This time they do not come back on. Within a few minutes the water turns lukewarm, then cold.

I take a quick mental inventory. There's a towel on the towel rack. My jeans and shirt are on the floor, bathrobe and gown on the tank behind the toilet. Holding onto the towel rack, I step out of the tub and grab the towel. I wrap it around myself, pick up my clothes and follow the wall out to the main room.

I'll call the desk, find out what's wrong. If there's no electricity, maybe they'll bring me a flashlight. Or a candle.

I work my way around the bed and pick up the hotel phone. There's a steady hum. I jiggle the disconnect button, but nothing happens. I let the wet towel slide to the floor, sit on the edge of the bed and get into my clothes.

In movies, the killer always cuts the telephone wire before he breaks down the door. But I have my cell. I can still call 911 if I have to.

I pick up my cell and touch the center button. It lights up. There's enough light that I can see my way to the door. The carpet beneath my feet is wet.

The locks are secure. The door is a heavy metal one.

The phone dims. I hit the button again and walk over to the desk. A Gideon Bible is lying there, open to Psalm 107: "Such as sit in darkness and in the shadow of death, being bound in affliction ..."

The cell phone light goes out again, and I wonder how much charge is left on the battery. If I could just talk to Andy, I'd feel better. He's hundreds of miles away, and he can't help me, but I touch the center button again. Contacts. Select #2.

He picks up on the sixth ring. "Kylie?" he asks.

"I couldn't sleep. I wanted to talk to you." It feels so good to hear his voice.

"What time is it?"

"It's past midnight."

"I was asleep," he says. "Is everything okay?"

"Yes. I missed my flight to Fayetteville, but they got me a later one. There was this strange man in the lobby. I couldn't understand what he said."

"What do you mean, strange man? Was he drunk?"

"No, I don't think so. He just acted weird. Like he wanted me to invite him to my room. Maybe he was drunk."

"Kylie, where are you?"

"Fayetteville. The Days Inn. I left my schedule on the fridge."

"And you're in your room? What happened to the man?"

"He went away. I'm okay."

"What kind of place is this?"

"It's just a hotel. It was dark when I got here, so I couldn't tell much about it. I don't think it's in the nicest part of town."

"Kylie, I want you to pack up and get out of there."

"Oh, Andy, I'm fine. There are four locks on the door."

"Kylie?"

"Yes?"

"Was this man trying to pick you up? Could he have thought ... What were you wearing?"

I look at the metal door, and I think of the man standing on the sidewalk outside the hotel, the rain on his shoulders, the look on his face. I think of Andy, at home in our bed, sitting up against the headboard, holding the phone to his ear.

What does he think I was wearing? A low-cut blouse and a push-up bra? There's a crackling on the line, and I wait for it to clear before I answer.

What was I wearing? I got dressed this morning while you were still in bed, I should tell him. I put on my jeans and T-shirt while you were sound asleep. I sat in the bedroom chair that was a wedding present from your aunt, and I put on my socks and shoes. I sat in that chair because I didn't want to wake you up. I did my makeup in the bathroom with the door closed so the light wouldn't disturb you. I closed my suitcase and carried it to the front door so you could get a few extra minutes of sleep before I woke you.

"I'm wearing the same clothes I wore this morning," I tell him. "The clothes I was wearing when you drove me to the airport, only now they're wet and dirty." The crackling has ended, but I'm not sure if he heard me or not. "I'm sorry, Andy. There's a storm outside. Lightening probably hit a tower. Are you still there?"

Yes, he's there, but his voice is breaking up. "Call the desk ... Kylie ... throw everything ... suitcase ... get out of there."

Whatever anger I felt at his words melts away. I tell my husband everything is okay, really it is, and I begin to tell him about the horse in Lancaster County. Even as I'm telling the story, I regret having brought it up. I don't want to have to answer questions about what the outcome might be. So I rush on. I describe the Amish community and the wonderful strawberry milkshake I had. I tell him about the Hostetler family and how they read the Bible by candlelight. I chatter on about how Mrs. Hostetler makes the clothes for her family, and she probably makes the candles as well.

At some point I realize there's no one on the other end. Andy isn't there. The connection has been lost. I hit the redial number, but the phone won't ring through.

There are only a few more hours of darkness. Then it will be morning. I have interviews scheduled at two clinics. I'll wear the only other outfit I brought with me: navy slacks, white blouse, London Fog jacket. I'll pull my hair back in a pony tail. I'll wear simple pearl earrings, a touch of pink lipstick.

For now, there's nothing to do but get under the covers and try to get some sleep. Tomorrow, when I'm finished with the interviews, I'll drive back to Raleigh, turn in the rental car, and fly home to Andy.

The colleges and universities within driving distance of the Cape Fear River Valley were never a good fit for Andy, but there's one in Missouri interested in hiring a Wildlife Biologist. He'd be perfect for the job. And surely I'll be able to find a position close by.

TATTER: (V) TO MAKE RAGGED

THERE'S A LITTLE GIRL sitting in the corner of the surgery. She smells of smoke and urine. She's wearing a thin night-gown, no shoes, no slippers. Her face is tear-streaked and dirty, her eyes red and swollen.

I have no time to ask about her, why she's in the room where we do our surgeries, or who brought her to the Hickory Valley Animal Clinic this early in the morning.

A fire truck has pulled up outside. Two firemen jump out, motor left running, doors swung wide. Someone opens the clinic door, and the firemen rush in. Each is carrying a cat, one bundled in an ice pack, the other pressed against the fireman's chest.

They take both patients into my examining room.

The cats are lying side by side on the table when I enter. The smell of smoke is strong. From the men and from the cats.

For a second I'm back at Texas A&M Animal Hospital, a fourth-year vet student on duty in the ICU. There had been a barn fire at the Equestrian Park. Sixteen horses died. Twenty-five others were brought to our facility. Most of them died within a few days.

"We pulled them out of an apartment over in Richland Heights," the lead fireman says. "Someone said to bring them here. Are you a vet?"

The cats are flat out. There are no burns that I can see, but no signs of life, either. With a nod of my head I indicate the newly framed degree my husband hung on the wall a month ago. "I'm Dr. Wheeler. Where's the owner?"

I'm clearing the soot and mucous from their nasal passages, checking for swelling or other obstructions in their throats, hoping for signs of life, when one of them takes a shuddering breath. For this one, at least, there's hope.

The walls were bare for the first few months I worked here. Then I put up a picture I'd had since high school of a Denali timber wolf. Later I added a print of Copycat, the famous cloned tabby, sitting in a teacup. Half the girls in my class at A&M wanted to adopt the kitten, just so she'd have a normal life instead of spending her days in a cage at a research lab.

The girls wanted her, but not the boys. Texas boys, especially Texas boys training to be veterinarians, are something else.

Two months ago, Andy, who is not a Texan, put up a laser copy of my DVM degree. He insisted we keep the original in the hallway of our new house. The remaining wall in my examining room is taken up with cupboards, counter space, a sink, various medical supplies.

"They belong to someone who lives in the complex," the lead fireman says. "The apartment they came out of is a total loss. Four units gone, but no fatalities." He looks down at the cats. "No human fatalities," he adds.

"The woman who owns them is a nurse," the other fireman says. "She wanted us to give them oxygen, but we didn't have the equipment. She thought you might be able to save them. Her sister works here, she told us."

One of the cats is dead.

The other has a heartbeat. Barely. Her temp is low, 95 degrees. I remove the ice pack and begin the process of starting fluids and oxygen. "Tell me where you found them," I ask. "Were they together? How close were they to the fire?"

As I work, I'm aware of the little girl, standing just beyond the doorway. She's still a baby, really, no more than two or three years old.

The men look at each other, as if each is expecting the other to provide answers to my questions.

"Was there carpet? Did they have access to oxygen? Did they try to get away from the fire? Tell me everything you can remember."

I'm grasping at straws. I've never treated a cat suffering from smoke inhalation before. I need help.

But there's no one to help me. I'm here alone. It'll be at least a half-hour before any of the other vets arrive.

"Someone carried them out of the building," the second fireman says. "That's all we know." He stops. The little girl has inched her way into the room.

"Tatter," she says. She's looking at one of the cats.

"Is this your cat?" I ask.

She nods. "She sleeps with me." She reaches up to touch the cat that is closest to her—the one that is still alive.

"Where's your mother?" I ask.

She shakes her head back and forth. "Don't know," she says, wiping a grimy hand across her cheek.

The taller fireman picks her up. "Who brought you here?" he asks. He's taken off his hat to reveal thick white hair. "Can you tell us?"

"Win," she says. She turns away from him so she can see the cats.

"Win?" he repeats. Eyebrows raised in puzzlement, he looks to me for an answer.

"Gwynne," I tell him. "She works here. She's one of our technicians."

He looks at the child. "Gwynne?" he asks. "Is that who you mean? Is she your aunt? Did she bring you here?"

"Win," she says, and she nods again. "She went to help Mommy. She said she'd come back for me."

"We'll help you find them," the fireman says, "Aunt Gwynne and your mother." With a last glance at the cats, he carries the child out to the waiting room. The second fireman follows.

Smoke inhalation victims often look good when they first come in. The patient is breathing, but the body is pouring fluid. The lungs fill up. It takes a day or two, maybe even three. For much of that time you can't tell them apart from a healthy animal. Then it all crashes. That is what I expect will happen with this cat. Tatter.

Her breathing is raspy and hoarse, her heartbeat thready. I pick her up and carry her to the recovery room. She's limp in my arms.

Gwynne arrives with a change of clothes for the little girl. She checks on Tatter, then makes up a pallet in a corner of my office.

The cats are litter mates, she tells me. Rags and Tatter are their names. They're three years old. Her sister adopted them from the St. Louis Humane Society when they were kittens.

Is it okay if Zoe, her niece, sleeps in my office until her mother gets here? The little girl has been awake since before dawn.

"Of course it is," I tell her. "Make sure there's nothing in there to hurt her."

"Beth, my sister, promised Zoe she'd go back for the cats," Gwynne says. "But once she got close, she knew it wasn't possible. She could never have gotten through."

"How were they rescued?"

"Someone went in through the back." She sighs. "Tatter doesn't have much of a chance, does she?"

She turns away before I can formulate an answer.

There's a Saturday morning crush of clients to attend to, the waiting room having filled up while I did what I could for the two cats. It's a relief to see patients who need vaccinations, examinations, incisions checked, blood drawn. I don't want to think about the cats that were trapped inside a burning apartment.

JAVMA, the Journal of the American Veterinary Medical Association, published a story on the fire at the College Station

Equestrian Park a few months after it happened. The authors presented theories as to why the kidneys fail after an animal has been in a fire. Is it because the animal has breathed in so many toxins from the smoke and the fire, and these toxins have to be filtered through the kidneys? Or that the kidneys have been heated up and can no longer function as they should? Or is it because the muscles break down, and all those waste products have to be filtered? Much of the article was written in technical terms, but you could feel the emotion in it.

Maybe I felt it more than most because I was on my ICU rotation when it happened, and a large part of my job was to care for the horses that came out of the barn fire. Six of them were brought to our ICU. We ended up euthanizing four of them. The smoke had wrecked their lungs.

One of the horses that survived belonged to a classmate, Drucie Renshaw, a third-year student from Austin. The horse was a black saddlebred with severe burns on his back and one of his legs. We thought a timber might have fallen on him.

We had no way of knowing how he'd gotten out of the fire, but somehow, he had. After three days in the ICU his lungs seemed to be okay and his kidneys were functioning. The burns on his back, though, were the worst we'd ever seen.

Drucie kept him in the ICU for as long as she could. We had the space by then, and she wanted to make sure he got the attention he needed.

We did skin graft after skin graft on that horse. Drucie would take him home, give him time to heal, then bring him back. Again and again and again. Her family poured thousands of dollars into him.

We all began to wonder why. It was such a hopeless case, yet Drucie seemed determined beyond all reason. It got so bad, it took four men to get him out of the trailer. The horse had learned to associate excruciating pain with being loaded and unloaded.

Did she ever think about what she was putting the horse through? Why couldn't she see what she was doing to him?

No one would ever be able to ride him again. This was Texas, and the horse was useless here.

Why did she do it? What was driving her?

My hands still smell of smoke when I get home that afternoon. I notice it when I get into my car. I go back inside the clinic and scrub until I'm certain the smell is gone.

But it isn't.

I wash them again when I get home. There's a park behind our house, and I'm standing at the kitchen sink, soaping my hands and forearms, looking out the window, when Andy comes up behind me. There are women pushing baby strollers, kids tossing Frisbees, couples out for an afternoon walk.

"It's wrong to not be aware of suffering," I say to Andy. "It's wrong to be happy and not acknowledge how much animals suffer."

"What are you talking about?" His arms are around me, and he's gently rocking me.

I disentangle myself, begin to dry my hands.

"We have no right to be happy without being aware of how much animals suffer."

"You're not making any sense, Kylie. Tell me what happened."

"They brought two cats into the clinic that were in that apartment fire this morning over in Richland Heights," I answer. "One was dead, and I killed the other one."

There, I've said it. I've told him. Now he'll say something that will give me some perspective on what's happened. He'll help me find a way out of this awful place where I've gone. I can count on him for that. He loves me.

"Stop it, Kylie. Tell me what really happened."

"I just told you."

"No, you didn't."

"One of the cats was dead when they brought her in. I killed the other one."

"Rephrase," Andy tells me, his voice somewhere between stern and angry.

"I euthanized the other one."

"Keep talking. Tell me more. Tell me why."

"I told the owner the cat had a ten percent chance of surviving. Beth Farnsworth. That's her name. She's a nurse. She asked me to be honest with her, to give it to her straight. She said she'd had burn patients at the hospital, and she knew what it was like. She didn't want to see the cat suffer."

"And?"

"It was my best estimate. Ten to fifteen percent. She sat by the cage, holding her daughter, trying to decide what to do. There are just the two of them. Beth is a single mom, and she lost everything she owned in the fire.

"I tried to find some place to transfer the cat, some facility that would offer better treatment than I could. But everywhere I called wanted at least $500 before they'd admit the cat. She didn't have the money. She couldn't pay the bill at the clinic. I knew I was doing it for free. That didn't matter. She's Gwynne's sister."

I walk into the dining room, stand by the glass doors that look out onto that same park, at those same kids, young mothers, couples. "I don't want to talk about it anymore."

The kids are running and shouting as they play. When the mothers finish their walks, they'll take their children back to homes with well-stocked kitchens, decorated nurseries, and comfortable living rooms. Some will hire babysitters, go out to dinner with their husbands, and hold hands beneath the table.

None of them will give a thought to what happened today.

"I want to see the apartment building where it happened," I tell Andy. "I'd like to drive over to Richland Heights, to see how bad it was."

"What good will it do? How is it gonna help?"

"I don't know. But I want to do it."

He gazes at me for a long time, then picks up the car keys from the counter and closes his fingers around them. He's worrying his bottom lip in that mannerism that tells me he's not certain what to do, that he needs time to think.

"Her name was Tatter," I tell him. "She was sitting up, looking at me, when I went to get her out of the cage."

He turns away so I can't see his face.

I had come to euthanize her, and she looked better. She got to her feet and looked at me, and it hit me then, what had happened. She was in shock when the fireman brought her in, and I got her out of it. She was doing better.

I stood there by the cage, smelling the smoke, shaking inside, finding it hard to breathe. I couldn't go back to the owner and tell her the cat was looking better. "Give it to me straight," Beth had said. "I'm a nurse. I've had smoke inhalation cases. Tell me what her chances are."

It was too late to go back to the owner. What could I say to her? That the cat had miraculously improved? That her chances now were twenty or twenty-five percent?

She'd agonized over the decision. She sat with the cat, petted her, talked to her. I let her spend all the time she wanted.

In the end, when she finally made the decision, it seemed the right thing to do.

Now I stood by the cage, and it didn't seem so right anymore.

I thought about trying to keep the cat alive. Would it be possible to nurse her back to health and take her home with me?

I remembered Drucie Renshaw, the times she brought the horse back, the money, the pain. It got so bad we hated to see the trailer pull up outside the hospital. Here comes the skin graft, we'd say. We dreaded the treatments we knew were coming, the smells, the hopelessness of it all, the wild look in the horse's eyes. He didn't understand why it was happening, couldn't comprehend anything beyond the pain. We couldn't make him understand. We didn't understand ourselves.

Did even Drucie understand?

I grew to hate that rotation. I yearned for it to end. I wanted to go on to some other aspect of veterinarian medicine where there were happy endings. Send me into the humane shelters, the wildlife clinics, the Texas prison system. Assign me to radiology, anesthesiology, surgery.

Something was driving Drucie Renshaw that caused her to keep that horse alive, no matter what the cost.

I stood by the cage looking at Tatter. Then I did what I believed I had to do.

Now I wonder how much I was influenced by Drucie Renshaw. Did I disapprove of what she had done so much that I've swung too far in the opposite direction?

Wisps of smoke are still rising from the apartment building when we get there. Andy parks beside the road, and we walk to the front of the complex. Orange barrels block the driveway. The burned-out building is surrounded by yellow tape.

The windows are blackened, the roof partially collapsed, the siding smoke-streaked. Odd bits of clothing, paper, and debris are scattered about. There's a child's tennis shoe in a ruined flower bed. Andy points to a wedding photograph, the glass broken, the photo torn and soggy.

A cold wind is blowing, stirring the ashes, spreading them across the landscape like a coating of gray snow.

I stand looking at the complex, wondering which apartment belonged to Beth and Zoe, Rags and Tatter. There's no one around, no one to tell me the things I want to know.

I shouldn't have come.

Carbon monoxide is the leading cause of death in cases of smoke inhalation. All fires produce a certain amount of it.

I will never know the exact composition of the smoke from this fire. It depends on so many things: the products being burned, the temperature of the fire, the amount of oxygen available. A kitchen fire is different from one in a living room or a bedroom.

I don't know where the fire started. I don't know if the cats stayed together or if they separated. Did one hide in a closet? Did Tatter find someplace where she had a good supply of oxygen that lasted until she was rescued?

They were sisters, litter mates, three years old. Spayed at our clinic when they were eight months old.

I take one last look around. "Zoe, Beth's daughter, was in her bare feet at the clinic. I wonder if that was her tennis shoe."

"Let's go home," Andy says. He takes my hand, and we begin walking toward the car.

"Zoe wanted one of the kittens we have in the waiting room, the ones we're adopting out. Her mother told her they needed to wait a while."

He makes no comment.

No one will admit it was my fault. None of the other veterinarians in the practice, none of the technicians, no one will say I made a mistake. No one will say I was too quick to advise euthanasia. Not even my husband.

He tries to be helpful. "Don't think about it," he tells me. "Try not to dwell on it. It's done. There's nothing you can do about it."

"I made a mistake," I tell him.

"You did what any good vet would have done."

"No. I was wrong. She had a chance and I took it away from her."

"If you'd kept her alive for three days, you know what that would have meant."

He takes me by the shoulders. "Remember what you said, Kylie, what she looked like, how her throat and nose were full of soot, her mucous black." His voice is rising with each word. "You know what she would have gone through if you'd done anything other than what you did. You, of all people, know what that kind of death is like." He's gripping my shoulders. I can feel the heat of his breath, his frustration, and his pleading.

How long before he tires of trying to reason with me, of trying to convince me of something I do not believe?

Three days go by. The smell of smoke is gone from my hands, but when I shower in the morning I still scrub them as if I were about to perform surgery.

"We need a ritual," Andy says. He's pouring coffee as I walk into the kitchen. "I've been thinking about it. We need some kind of ceremony, a poem, a rite, something we can do that will honor the life that's gone." He slides a cup across the counter toward me.

I sit on the barstool, add cream to the coffee. "I remember a doctor who lived near where I grew up," I tell him. "Every time he lost a patient, he planted a tree. Soon his whole yard was filled up. You couldn't see the house for the jungle."

"What did he do then? Move to a bigger place?"

I nod. "To a house out in the country with a hundred acres."

"There was a purpose in what he did."

I run my finger around the top of the cup, thinking of that house hidden behind all that foliage, shaded by all those trees.

"We could use some juniper bushes out front," Andy says, sipping his coffee. "Later on, we might add some pyramidal trees at the corners of the house."

It's past midnight; we've been in bed since 10:30 p.m. The room is dark and close.

"You would be doubting yourself just as much if you'd done the opposite of what you did," Andy says. "You know that, don't you, Kylie?" He turns toward me, props his head on his elbow. "Kylie, are you awake? Did you hear what I said?"

"I wish I'd given her a chance."

"You're convinced she could have made it?"

"Yes. I don't know. Maybe. "

"What about the owner? You said she had experience in a burn unit. Don't you think she was doing her own assessment of the cat?"

"She was making a decision based on other things besides the condition of the cat."

"And you don't have that luxury."

I want Andy to understand. I want him to listen to me, and to hear what I'm trying to tell him. If he touches me, I won't be able to find the words.

I get up out of bed and walk to the window. "When the firemen brought her in," I tell him, "it didn't even occur to me that she was in shock. I just started working on her. I knew what I had to do and I did it. It was automatic, like the horses we treated at A&M. But back then I wasn't all alone. There were professors looking over my shoulder, making sure I did the right thing. I was all alone with this cat, and there was no one I could consult with." I part the curtains and look out onto that darkened park. "Hardly any of the horses survived," I continue. "Maybe I let that influence me."

"You have to move on, Kylie. There's nothing to be gained by going over it again and again. Somehow you have to learn to live with it."

"I don't know how."

He sinks back onto the mattress and is quiet for a time. Then he speaks into the darkness. "They say a doctor isn't really a doctor until he kills someone. Once he absolutely, unequivocally does something that causes a person's death, he makes some kind of mistake, he gives the wrong medicine or the wrong treatment, only then is he a doctor. "

Maybe I don't want to be a doctor, I think to myself.

"If you made a mistake," he goes on, "it's one you'll never make again."

I think about that, and the other things he's said. I let the curtain fall back into place, and I climb into bed. I feel comforted by his words.

When I wake in the morning, something inside me has changed.

I hear Andy in the kitchen. I put on my robe and pad down the hallway in my bare feet, slide onto the barstool. Elbows on counter, face cupped in my hands, I look at him. "What kind of pyramidal tree did you have in mind?" I ask.

"Whatever you want. A Nellie Stevens Holly would be nice. They get red berries on them in the wintertime. Maybe an Eastern Arborvitae. We'd need something that would thrive in part-shade."

"You'd plant two of them? One at each of the front corners of the house?"

He nods.

"I think I'd like that," I tell him.

"Are we starting a tradition?" he asks.

The sun is coming through the kitchen window behind him, and he looks warm and golden.

"No. But I'd like to do it, just this once."

TELL ME WHERE IT HURTS

THE CAT GLARES AT ME when I walk into the room. I approach the examining table, and he hisses. Sixteen pounds of black alley cat, he's ready for a fight. I can read his mind: Don't come any closer, Dr. Kylie Wheeler. I own this room.

I extend a hand, an offer of friendship. He hisses again. I notice a blackened canine tooth. And from his open mouth a wave of foul breath.

He seems not at all bothered by the fact that he's being held captive by his owners, a family of three who have brought him to the clinic. He must own them, too.

But not Gwynne, my technician, who's waiting for me to give her the signal. A nod of my head and she'll put him in a strangle hold. It's the only way I can do my job with a patient like this.

A third of the tooth has been broken off. Infection and gross swelling of the gum have caused the tooth to angle out, making it difficult for him to eat or even close his mouth.

The owners' story is a jumbled waterfall of behavior terrorism. "He attacks my legs for no reason," the woman says, "then runs out of the kitchen like he's being chased."

"Which he sometimes is," the father says.

"He was sleeping on my bed last night, and I petted him, and he bit me," the little boy says. "You wanna see?" He holds up a bandaged finger.

In addition to the abscess, there's evidence of advanced periodontal disease throughout his mouth. The cat is probably in excruciating pain.

"Bring him in early in the morning," I tell the owners. "I'll anesthetize him, remove the tooth, and give the rest of them a good cleaning. You can pick him up tomorrow afternoon."

"Will he be able to eat?" the boy asks. "If you take out his tooth?"

"Better than ever," I tell him. "And he'll turn into a nice cat again. I promise."

"Where did you get all those kittens you have in the cage? In the other room?"

"Someone left them on our doorstep a few days ago. Gwynne found them when she came to work."

"Can I have one?" he asks.

Gwynne appraises the boy and then looks at me. The movement of her head is barely perceptible.

"We already have a cat, son," the father says, taking him by the hand. "We don't need another."

"They're too young, anyway," I tell him. "They haven't learned to eat solid food yet."

"Are they all from the same litter?" the mother asks.

I shrug. "We don't know. They were in one big box, all eight of them. They're about the same size, so they could be from the same litter."

Except for the two who are smaller, I remember. Two of the eight are definitely runts of the litter. Or litters.

My next client is a repeat: I'd seen this white terrier the first week I began work at the Hickory Valley Animal Clinic. The dog, three years old, had suddenly begun having seizures. I suspected a brain tumor. I prescribed anti-seizure meds, and she'd responded well.

The client brought her back a week later. There'd been no more seizures; Tammy was her old, playful self. As the client was leaving, he turned to ask how long I'd been a vet. "You look so young," he said. His face colored, and he looked down at the dog in his arms.

"Oh, I graduated back in May," I answered, pleased that my voice was so airy and light.

He might have taken that to mean I'd been a vet for six months, but I hadn't said that. A more honest answer would have been that I'd been employed, at that point, for exactly three weeks. Gwynne, who was wiping down the examining table, risked a glance in my direction. Her eyes sparkled with mirth.

"I'd like you to be my regular vet," Mr. Ferguson said. "I'm so impressed with what you've done for my Tammy. The seizures were so awful."

"I can't promise they won't return."

"I understand. But I'd like to bring her to you, from now on, if that's okay."

And he has. Every three months, for more than a year. Tammy continues to do so well, I'm tempted to cut back on her medication. If the seizures were caused by something other than a tumor, a trauma perhaps, or a toxin ingestion, it might be possible to wean her off the meds.

But I look at Mr. Ferguson, and I see such trust in his eyes. I decide to play it safe.

"She's looking wonderful," I tell him. "You're doing a fine job taking care of her."

The cat I see that afternoon is very sick. She's been under treatment at our clinic for two years. Now she's in the final stages of renal failure.

I rest my hand lightly on her body and whisper her name. "Sushi."

She stirs, lifts her head, lets it drop back onto the table.

I offer to hydrate her, but the client refuses. I run through the options, suggesting what treatment I can, what little is left.

"I think it's time," the woman says.

I nod. "Would you like to stay with her?"

She shakes her head. "I don't think I could stand it."

I remember the James Herriot books I read when I was in high school. The stories all had happy endings. Even when he lost an animal, somehow he managed to make it come out all right.

"You're doing the right thing," I tell my client. "No one could have done any more for her than you did." I have a hard time looking at the woman because my eyes are burning, tears threatening, and that isn't very professional.

I've done it many times before. I'm good at this. I've lost track of how many animals I euthanized while I was in school. You can't get a DVM degree without euthanizing animals. Lots of them. Often we're better surgeons than medical doctors because we have so much hands-on experience.

I remember the baby goats when I was in my third year of vet school. They were the hardest. They wanted to lick our faces, and we let them until it was time to anesthetize them. We practiced our surgical techniques, all the while keeping careful watch on their vitals. When we were finished, we euthanized them and sent their bodies to the incinerator.

I tell my client the procedure I will follow. First the sedative to relax Sushi, help her fall asleep. Then the medication that will stop her heart.

I should ask about disposal of the remains. I look at the owner, wondering how to frame my question.

"I have to go," she says. She strokes the cat, leans down to kiss her, turns to leave.

"Would you like to come back later? Take her home?"

She shakes her head.

I'm alone with the cat, cradling her against my breast, waiting for Gwynne to come help me with the procedure.

Gwynne. How would I have gotten through those first few months in practice if it hadn't been for Gwynne? She was always there, to oh-so-carefully tell me what the other vets in the practice might do in similar circumstances, to clue me in on protocols different from what I learned in vet school, to run interference with the office manager when I neglected to include a charge.

The cat stirs in my arms. I take a deep breath, trying to get control.

If Herriot ever treated patients with chronic renal failure, he chose not to write about them. The disease is progressive and terminal. There are no happy endings.

"When will my golden retriever come into heat?" a client asks.

"There's really no set time. They can be as young as four months or as old as a year and a half."

"How often will she go into season? Will it be every six months?"

I don't know. They didn't teach us that in vet school. "It varies," I answer. "The best thing to do is watch her and let her tell you. Okay?"

I make a mental note to look it up when I go home this evening, so I'll be able to give a better answer next time someone asks.

"What about cats?" the client asks.

"Seven to nine months. It's good to get them spayed at about six months."

The question reminds me that I need to do some research on storage diseases. There's something wrong with those two kittens out in the reception room. The other six are fine, but the two little ones don't have the motor skills they should. The female in particular. When she looks at you, her head trembles. There's some kind of neurological problem, I'm convinced.

If it's viral, she'll have a chance. But if it's a storage disease, the inappropriate storage of waste products in the cerebellum, it will only get worse.

The woman grabs onto the side of the examining table to keep from falling. Gwynne puts a protective arm around the dog, poised to slide the animal away if the woman topples. The air in the room is sour with the smell of whiskey and cigarette smoke.

Squinting against the fluorescent lights, the woman sways, looking as if she might collapse.

The dog lies quiet and somber on the table, head resting on her paws, dark eyes alert. She's part shepherd, part something I can't identify, nine years old, 42 pounds, last seen six years ago.

The owner brought the animal to the clinic five minutes before closing time. Gwynne did the preliminary workup.

Glad for a reason not to look at the woman, I read the notes on the blue card and then glance through the dog's history. Puppy shots, a bout with diarrhea six years ago. No follow-up. No recent visits.

The woman has no money. She told me that when I first came into the room. What am I supposed to do about that, I wondered.

"I don't have any money," she says again. "My husband lost his job six months ago."

"We can work something out," I tell her, wondering exactly what we can work out. I'm expected to bring in enough revenue to cover my salary and a portion of the office expenses. There are months when I fall woefully short.

I can feel the practice manager watching me, disapproving of how I do my job. I spend too much time with patients, he says. I need to work more efficiently, see more patients, learn to utilize the vet techs for procedures I'm used to doing myself.

But practicing vet medicine is not like working on an assembly line. The patients I see need me to heal whatever has gone wrong. My job is to do that, and to take away their pain, if I can. They may be scared, and they may fight me, but I can't ever lose sight of my goal: to help them live the best lives possible.

The client pushes her hair back, hooks it behind her ears. "It's hot in here, isn't it?" she asks.

I look at Gwynne. Don't leave me alone with this woman, I silently plead.

"I lost a dog a month ago," the client says, wiping her eyes. "His name was Lincoln. We got him when he was a puppy. After he died, I started worrying that something might happen to Brown Dog. I told Tom I was gonna bring her to the vet. Just to make sure she was okay."

"What happened to your other dog? Lincoln?"

"Tom thought it was the hot weather. Tom's my husband. You know how dogs go off their feed sometimes in the summertime? It's awfully hot in here, isn't it?" She pulls her shirt away from her body, fans herself with the loose fabric. "He just quit eating," she says. "Then one day, about a month ago, I went out into the yard, and there he was. Dead. Under the lilac bush."

I put the stethoscope to Brown Dog's chest and listen to her heart, lungs, and abdominal sounds. The owner chatters on. Gwynne will let me know if she says anything important.

The dog has never been spayed. I tell the woman unspayed females are likely to get breast tumors.

"She never goes out of the yard," the woman says.

I'm not surprised when I find a tumor along the mammary gland chain, only that I found it two seconds after warning the woman of the danger. Located near the dog's back legs, it's an inch in diameter, hard, firmly attached to deeper tissue structures. I glance at my watch. It's already ten after six. Andy will be home from work by now, probably starting dinner. He planned to stop for a bottle of wine to celebrate our first wedding anniversary.

"I'm afraid your dog has a tumor," I tell the woman.

She slumps forward. "I knew there was something wrong with her," she says, her voice high and keening. "I knew in my bones. Something just told me."

"I'll need to aspirate it," I tell her.

She doesn't answer. Her eyes are closed, her lips moving as if in silent prayer.

I select a needle and begin the procedure. The dog raises her head and looks at me but does not move. "Good girl, Brown Dog," I tell her, hoping she doesn't sense the dread that is washing over me.

"There was no reason to have her spayed," the woman says, reviving, pushing back from the table. "We have a fenced-in backyard, and she never goes out. I didn't have to worry about her getting pregnant."

I could tell her that 26 percent of unspayed female dogs will at some point develop mammary tumors, and 45 percent of these will be cancerous. I might explain that the presence of female hormones promotes the growth of these tumors. That early spaying can significantly reduce the risk, and that spaying before the first, second, or third heat cycle is highly recommended.

But she's standing so close, and the whiskey on her breath is so strong, I don't say any of these things. I finish the procedure, leave Gwynne with the dog and the woman, and go back to examine the specimen under the microscope.

It looks like cancer, yet the cells are not typical. I can't be certain. Considering the age of the dog, the fact that she is unspayed, the feel of the tumor, the firm attachment of the nodule to the underlying tissue, I'm willing to go with a tentative diagnosis of cancer … knowing I could be wrong. Only a tissue biopsy will tell me with certainty.

I return to the examining room and recommend surgical removal of the tumor as a first step. Depending on the results of the biopsy, we can decide if further treatment is necessary.

"Further treatment?"

"If the cancer has spread to the lymph nodes, there are other things we can do."

"You mean radiation? Chemo? It didn't help my mother," she says.

"The first thing is to remove the tumor."

She covers her face with both hands and begins to weep. Brown Dog perks her ears, raises her head to look at her owner, whimpers.

The front door bell sounds. We hear footsteps in the waiting room.

"Tom," the woman cries, and she runs out to meet him.

We wait, Gwynne, the dog, and I, listening to their voices, muted at first, then loud and charged with emotion.

He's angry with his wife, angry at her tipsy condition, angry that she brought the dog to the clinic.

I go into the back room to look at the slide again. It bothers me that the specimen is not textbook, and that I can't be certain of the diagnosis. I should be able to identify a cancer cell. Fine needle aspiration biopsies can detect the presence of malignant cells with a fair degree of accuracy. Yet the longer I look at the slide, the more I begin to doubt myself.

Tom is alone by the examining table when I return.

"I'm sorry to have such bad news. About the dog. Is your wife okay? "

"Joanne," he says. "She went out to the car. The dog has cancer?"

"She has a nodule in the mammary gland chain. They're very common in unspayed females. I aspirated it, and it looks suspicious. My guess is, yes, she has cancer. I won't know for certain until we do a tissue biopsy, but the tumor should be removed, regardless. I would also recommend a hysterectomy. Research shows that even older dogs benefit from …"

"This is too much for my wife to deal with," he says. "I need to take her home. Put the dog down and send me the bill. I'll pay it when I can."

I take a deep breath. "It's quite possible I can remove the tumor and no further treatment will be necessary. We should spay her, of course. Even at this age, it's better …"

"How much would it cost?"

I look at Gwynne. "We can print out an estimate …"

"I mean euthanasia. Look, Dr. Wheeler, I don't have money for cancer treatments that probably won't work anyway. I want you to put the dog down."

"If I remove the tumor, and it hasn't spread …"

He moves toward the dog, begins to lift her from the table.

"I can do both surgeries at the same time. If it's metastasized, we'll have to … the charge for euthanasia is $60."

He hesitates. "I can take care of it myself for a lot less than that," he says.

I close my eyes and turn away from him, not wanting to imagine how he might take care of it. "I'll have to speak with your wife," I tell him. "She brought the dog in. I'll need her permission."

He walks out of the room, out of the building. A few minutes later he returns, Joanne by his side.

I look at her, and I know what she's going to say.

She's combed her hair. She stands straighter now, her head held high. She does not wobble like before. She carries a purse hooked over her left shoulder. Imitation leather or the real thing, I can't tell. I imagine the items that are inside: cigarettes, wallet, checkbook, credit cards, comb, lipstick, mascara, perfume, driver's license, sunglasses, mirror, pictures of children, perhaps grandchildren. These are the things she values. And she's about to tell me to euthanize the dog she's had for nine years.

"Tom thinks the best thing is to let you put Brown Dog to sleep," she says. "He says we can put her in a black plastic bag, and he'll carry her out to the car. He's promised to dig a grave for her in the backyard. That's where she's lived all her life, and she'd want to be buried there."

Tom reaches into his back pocket, takes out his wallet, extracts a bill folded to the size of a quarter.

It takes a long time for him to unfold it and smooth it out. When he's done, he holds it out to me.

Before I leave the clinic that night I call Andy. "I'm still here," I tell him.

"Tough case?" he asks.

"Yes. A tough one."

"Last-minute client?"

"We were ready to close when she came in."

"You had to handle it by yourself?"

I don't answer.

"An accident?" he asks.

"No, not exactly."

He's quiet for a time. "Savannah called," he says. "Your friend from vet school. She wanted to talk to you."

"Is she here?"

"No. She's in Seattle."

"I'll call her when I get home."

"Dinner's in the oven. Can you tell me? About the case?"

"No. I don't want to talk about it."

"I made a veggie casserole. With tofu. I'll keep it warm."

"Why don't you go ahead and eat? I'm not very hungry. I'd just like to come home and go to bed."

"Kylie, tell me what happened."

"I had to put a dog down."

"Are you alone?"

"I mishandled it from the beginning."

I hear him take a deep breath and slowly exhale. The phone feels heavy in my hand. "Gwynne left a few minutes ago. She stayed late. To help me."

"I'll drive down and pick you up."

For a second I'm tempted. For many seconds. I think what it would feel like to melt into his arms and let him hold me, to rest my head against his chest until it all dissolves and there are just the two of us, alone in our house, the door closed to the world.

My car is in the parking lot. I'd have to leave it overnight, and the clinic is not in the best neighborhood. "No, I'm okay," I tell him. "I have some things to finish up here. Then I'll be home."

"It'll be dark soon."

"I'll be home as soon as I can."

I reach into my pocket, retrieve my wedding ring and slip it on.

I check that the medicine cabinets are secure, dim the lights, set the alarm. Before I walk out the door, I glance at the cage where the kittens are sleeping. For a moment

I consider grabbing the two little ones and taking them home with me for the night. I wonder if Andy would see what I see: the slight tremors in their heads, their lack of coordination, the weakness in their hindquarters. But it's late, I have tons of research to do, and there would be little time for me to observe them.

I lock the outside door and walk to my car.

I should never have mentioned the possibility of cancer to that woman. It might have gone differently if I'd never brought up cancer.

I hit the button that unlocks the driver's door.

If I'd been more certain of the diagnosis, I'd feel better about it.

I get into the car and start the engine.

I might have talked the woman, drunk as she was, into authorizing surgery if I hadn't used that word. Lumpectomy, regional or radical mastectomy, a concurrent ovario-hys-terectomy would have been optimal, but I wouldn't have pushed that. I could have skipped the vaccinations, some of the other fees.

I put the car in reverse, back around, and pull out onto Laurel Wood Drive.

You have to please the client. They taught us that in vet school. The client pays the bill.

Gwynne saw I wasn't going to take the $20 bill he was holding out to me. If she hadn't intervened, taken the money and gone to get him a receipt, I might have told him to put it back in his pocket.

But she took it, and that was that.

I knew what she was doing. She was trying to tell me I had no choice. You can't be a bleeding heart for every poor son-of-a-bitch who walks through the door. You can't save every animal that comes to you.

Yet Gwynne is often the softest touch in the office. She wants to adopt the two kittens, knowing there's something wrong with them. She has five cats already; there's no way she can afford to care for these two. But she wants them.

If Andy hasn't already opened the wine, I'll ask him to put it back in the fridge. We can save it for another occasion.

When my research for the night is done, I often go into the internet chat room set up by the university for our class. We talk about our experiences, share case studies, give advice, sometimes laugh, sometimes rage, and sometimes cry.

At one time or another we all visit there, each of us who walked across the stage that May afternoon, received our doctoral hoods, and stood before the dean for the conferral of our DVM degrees. Together we recited the oath that bound us to a lifetime of work to benefit society, to relieve animal suffering, to promote public health, and to advance medical knowledge. We accepted as a lifelong obligation the continual improvement of our professional knowledge and competence.

Today I euthanized a dog that did not need to be euthanized.

Worse things have happened to some of my classmates. Back in July, Savannah did routine vaccinations on a golden retriever puppy. The client called the next morning. The dog was dead. They found him on the kitchen floor when they got up.

Jeremy, one of the smartest people in our class, was repairing a neck wound on a patient when he nicked the carotid artery. The animal bled to death in less than a minute. There was nothing he could do.

Will it get easier, I wonder? As I become more experienced, more familiar with the routines, will I begin to feel comfortable in this profession? Will the time come when I have confidence in my decisions and diagnoses?

My first week on the job was awful. I was absolutely overwhelmed. What needle should I use for canine rabies shots? Feline leukemia? What vaccines do they normally give in this practice on the banks of the Mississippi? At what age? Why did Dr. Sussman, with whom I share an office, not offer treatment for the dog diagnosed with heartworms?

Nothing prepared me for the number of euthanasias I'd have to do, nor for the fact that every other client seemed to have just lost his job. I began to wonder if I'd made a mistake in choosing to work in a blue-collar practice.

Yet I know I'm becoming more competent as a veterinarian. Even in the relatively short time I've been here my declaws have improved. If I'm not able to talk my clients out of declawing, and I always try, at least I'm doing a better job with the procedure now. My incisions are smaller, and the wounds heal quicker. I send the cats home with plenty of pain medication. Is it foolish of me to think they understand, and that they don't hold me responsible?

I wonder how many of these new kittens in the cage in the waiting room I'll have to declaw. Another week and we can start giving them away.

I pull into the driveway of our split-level house and look up at the living room windows. The light from our torch lamp is shining out onto the stone walkway and into the yard. Andy is waiting for me.

Storage diseases in felines are as rare as they are in humans; only about one in five thousand is affected. Symptoms include head tremors, neurological dysfunction, mild ataxia. Storage diseases are progressive, inexorable, and deadly. Children diagnosed with these diseases rarely live past their teens.

It's two in the morning, and I'm sitting at my computer, logged into VIN, the Veterinary Information Network. The website provides a wealth of information on just about any subject having to do with veterinary medicine: clinical and research studies, treatment options, pharmaceuticals, disease information and outbreaks, professional support. It's where I go for help with difficult cases.

At any time of the day or night there are hundreds of veterinarians logged in, discussing their cases. They are insomniacs, seekers of knowledge, troubled souls who want to provide the best for their patients. Tonight I am one of them.

Rain splatters heavily on the skylight above my head, but Andy is sound asleep. He did not stir when I slipped out of bed and went into the den.

Storage diseases, and there are a number of them, come from a recessive gene. You would expect 25 percent of a litter to be affected. Two kittens from a litter of eight is 25 percent. It's an interesting coincidence.

For reasons we do not completely understand, the brain is unable to get rid of certain substances manufactured in the cerebellum. The resulting intracellular storage causes progressive physical and/or mental deterioration. The symptoms become more and more pronounced and severe. In time the disease will completely destroy the cerebellum.

I print out several articles. This is a case I would like to present at our next staff meeting. The kittens are strictly speaking not our patients, but someone brought them to our clinic, and we have an obligation to care for them.

I log out of the VIN website and sit at my desk, listening to the rain, thinking about the two kittens. I pick up the pages I printed and thumb through them until I find the sentence I'm searching for. "Because of the nature of neurologic storage diseases, the early onset, and the ultimate resolution, very little research has been done on them."

A Google search tells me what I want to know: the head of neurological research at the University of Ohio College of Veterinary Medicine is Dr. Elizabeth Reynolds. She was one of my teachers at Texas A&M. I make a note of her phone number and clip it to the articles.

I wonder if she'd be interested in taking the two kittens.

They become known in the office as the neurologic kittens. No two subjects were ever more closely observed. Everyone on staff is an expert: there are discussions among the vets, techs, receptionists, and practice manager. Is there really something wrong with these kittens? Or are they just slow to develop? Could they have some viral disease that will resolve on its own?

My VIN papers are passed around, discussed, argued over. There are debates as to whether or not their symptoms are getting worse. Dr. Vandevere, one of the owners of the practice, swears the male kitten has no head tremors, though he can clearly see them in the female. "That would argue against it being a genetic disease, if it's one litter and not two or three," he says.

"It could be two litters of four, so if just one has the disease, that's still 25 percent," the receptionist says.

"We should call them something other than neurologic kittens," I say.

Dr. Vandevere looks at me but does not answer.

It's a chilling word, neurologic. Too often it means there's nothing we can do. In a more upscale practice we could test, experiment, refer, any number of things. But here on the banks of the Mississippi our resources are limited.

Every Thursday night the staff meets to discuss unusual or difficult cases, protocols, new developments, changes in our practice we want to implement. Pain management is a constant item on our agenda. Because I'm the youngest member of the staff and the newest graduate, the other three vets look to me to come up with a recommendation.

I spend hours at home on my computer reading research papers. I email classmates, my old professors, experts in the field, trying to find out what works best in what circumstances, which meds are most cost-effective. Our goal is to send every surgical patient home with adequate pain medication, and to educate our clientele about the need for it.

We spend very little time during the meeting discussing the neurologic kittens. "They're your problem," Dr. Vandevere tells me, sliding my research papers across the table to me. "You decide what to do with them."

The six siblings have been adopted, replaced with three orphans. A client found them in a gas station garbage container two blocks away and brought them to our clinic.

The meeting continues. I present an argument against using the FIV vaccine. It protects against only two of the five strains, and those two are not the most prevalent. If the cat is ever tested again, she'll come up positive because of the vaccine, regardless of whether she has the disease or not. If she ends up in a shelter, they'll test and immediately euthanize.

I do not prevail.

Before the meeting breaks up, I bring up the question of heartworms. Why do we sometimes offer treatment and sometimes not? What are the criteria?

"If the heartworms are in the larvae stage, not well-established," Dr. Sussman says, "you can bet it's a new infection. Often times you can control it with Heartgard alone."

Immature heartworm larvae can molt into adult heartworms within two months, I want to tell him. How can you be certain the blood test didn't miss the mature ones? But I let it go.

"Then too," Dr. Sussman continues, "you have to consider the finances of the client. And how much they're willing to do for the dog."

There it is again.

Yet I know what he means. The cost of treating is at least $500. It involves risk. The dog must be confined for a period of three months. He must be closely monitored, and his activity severely restricted.

Dr. Sussman's answer presents another question to research when I get home. Will Heartgard really keep heartworms, even a new infection, under control?

My classmates provide the answer: Heartgard treatment is clearly not aggressive, but it is standard in many practices. "We do what we can in an imperfect world," Jeremy messages me.

"Try to keep your puppy from coming into contact with other dogs, at least until he's a few months older."

My patient is a fluffy yellow Lab, six weeks old. Like the vet school goats, he wants to lick my face, my hands. He's so rambunctious it's nearly impossible to examine him.

"There are a lot of dogs around where I live," the client says. He's an old man, shabbily dressed, but clearly in love with his new puppy. "I live in a trailer park."

"Maybe you could find a corner for him? Away from other dogs?"

He looks doubtful.

I mark the charge sheet lightly, forgetting to charge for half of what I've done. I give him all the free Purina Puppy Chow I can find. Then I hand him a booklet on the care of new puppies and an instruction sheet that describes the shots he'll need.

He leafs through the booklet, then looks at the instruction sheet.

"I'll let you keep these, Doctor," he says, handing them back to me.

"Are you sure? There's lots of information about puppies, how to feed them, their shots, reactions they might have. Are you sure you don't want them? There's no charge."

"I can't read," he says.

I take the packet and watch as he lifts his dog off the table.

"I'll bring him back in three weeks, like you said."

"He's a nice dog. He's gonna make a nice pet for you."

He nods and shuffles out to the waiting room to pay his bill.

There's always a new client waiting with a new set of problems, a new challenge. Sometimes the diagnosis and treatment plans are easy, but too often I'm dissatisfied with my performance. It frustrates me when I don't have the answers. I try to hide my disapproval of owners who won't let me test and treat or follow my hunches.

A woman brings me a cat that was spayed at our clinic. "She's in heat," the client says. "She was spayed and now she's in heat."

"That's not possible," I tell her, looking at the chart. The cat's name is Gypsy. Her surgery, two months ago, was unremarkable.

The woman insists. "Doctor, I grew up with cats," she says. "I know the behavior. Squatting with her rear end up in the air, tail off to the side, rubbing up against furniture, there's no mistaking it. Gypsy is in heat."

I consult with both Drs. Sussman and Vandevere. It isn't possible, they tell me. It simply isn't possible. But Sussman seems distracted. He did the surgery—there it is on the chart—but he can't specifically remember it. He begins to walk away.

"Was there anything unusual about her anatomy?" I ask. "Anything at all?"

He glares at me. "I've done thousands of spays," he says. End of conversation.

I start back to the examining room, but he follows me down the hall, puts his hand on my arm. "I remember a case where there was only one ovary," he says. "It was a couple of months ago. It might have been this one."

"I've never heard of a cat with only one ovary," I answer, and instantly regret my words.

He lets go of my arm and walks away.

The client is waiting. There's nothing I can do but go back in, offer to repeat the surgery.

I must have done a hundred shelter spays when I was in school. Maybe two hundred. In my final semester we fixed every mature cat brought into the Houston Animal Shelter. Feral cats that did not have a clipped left ear, indicating they'd already been fixed, were either spayed or neutered. I know the procedure. You explore until you find an ovary, remove it, follow the horn down to its base at the top of the uterus, follow the second horn up to the second ovary. Every uterus I've ever seen has two horns, each with its own ovary. Sussman must have missed the second ovary.

"This cat is in season," the woman tells me as soon as I walk back into the room. "I couldn't sleep last night for the yowling. This morning there were four cats at my back door. It's a sliding glass door. They were taking turns looking in. Four male cats. There's no mistaking it, Dr. Wheeler. Gypsy is in heat."

I promise to do some research and call her the next day.

I call Savannah as soon as I get home from work. She's my best friend in the world, my lab partner in vet school, maid of honor at my wedding.

Savannah works at a feline-only clinic in Seattle. Someone in her practice has heard of a case like this. "Get on your computer," Savannah says. "I'll send you a link."

A vet practicing in rural South Carolina once had a problem like this one, I learn. Somehow, during the surgery, he missed an ovary. Maybe the cat was spayed too young, maybe one of the ovaries was smaller than it should have been. He never knew. He excised what he thought was the proper tissue and closed.

The client was back two months later. Something was wrong. The cat had no uterus, could never get pregnant, but would cycle in and out of heat until the problem was corrected. The only solution was to have the client bring the cat back in at the first sign of heat, the veterinarian advised. "When you open her up, the ovary will be all swollen and red. You can't miss it."

I sit at my computer and laugh. Bring the cat back in. Mystery solved. I make a note to call the client in the morning.

Flea allergies, annual exams, hypothyroidism, cataracts, joint pain. I see a puppy with diarrhea, and I prescribe antibiotics. He's back a week later. More antibiotics. After they've gone, it occurs to me I should have prescribed ID dog food. I forgot.

There's a dog with several broken teeth on the right side of his jaw. I should have suggested surgery, but one look at the owner and I knew he wouldn't have gone for it.

"It doesn't seem to bother him," the old man said.

"I would imagine it's pretty painful," I answer.

"How much do you think it hurts?"

"I don't know how much it hurts. He could be experiencing excruciating pain every time he bites down on a piece of food."

"He doesn't act like he's hurting. You should see how he eats."

Spay infection, temp of 105.4. I prescribe pain medication and antibiotics.

I take a phone call from a client, and I struggle to remember who she is, what did her cat look like, what was the problem. Then I place her, and I grip the phone a little tighter. It's the feline leukemia cat I saw yesterday morning.

"He's beginning to eat," the woman tells me, and the excitement in her voice is wonderful to hear. "He actually walked into the kitchen this morning and cried, like he was hungry."

I remember that I'd started him on a couple of meds in case he has hemobartonellosis (feline infectious anemia) in addition to FeLV. It was a shot in the dark, but it worked. The owner is thrilled that her cat is feeling better.

A man brings in a beautiful, long-haired black cat, three years old. Black cats are my weakness. I love them.

I pull back his lips to look at his gums. They're pure white. He must have no red blood cells in his body. Leukemia. He does not have long to live, no matter what I do.

The owner tells me he has eight other cats at home. They've all been exposed. "Feline leukemia," I tell him. "FeLV. It's contagious, a retrovirus spread through shared food and water bowls, saliva, nasal secretions, urine, feces, blood. There's no danger to humans. But the other cats … we can vaccinate the youngest ones. The vaccine is 90 to 95 percent effective. Keep them all indoors, if you can. Bring them in, one by one. I'll do what I can."

This is a case that will be with me for a long time. I won't be able to walk away from this one. I will take it home with me, and it will keep me awake at night.

And in the end, it will surely break my heart.

Ryan Beckett, a new client at the practice, brings in a black Labrador. The receptionist shows him into my examining room.

Beckett wears the uniform of the rising young professional: slick gray suit, ocean blue tie with silver threads running through it, starched white shirt. Stock broker, lawyer, financial advisor, or health-care executive, I judge.

"He's a stray," Beckett says. "He showed up at my house a few months ago." He hands the leash to Gwynne. "I don't really want to spend any money on him."

"Labs are terrible roamers," I tell him. "Let me check to see if he's been microchipped. You've had him how long?"

"A few months. Five or six, maybe. He just appeared on my porch one morning. No collar, nothing to tell who owned him. I call him Ben."

The dog is young and healthy, his eyes bright, his coat glossy. There is no microchip.

Unwilling to pay for shots for a dog that does not belong to him, Beckett only wants something for the diarrhea.

I always want to test. I want to run every test I possibly can, because that's what I learned in vet school. The obscure diseases are still fresh in my mind, and I find them often enough to justify the cost.

But Beckett is adamant: no vaccinations, no tests. The dog does not belong to him.

"I should rule out parasites," I tell him, "at the very least."

He isn't interested.

I prescribe Pepto-Bismol, cooked rice, a round of antibiotics, and ID dog food.

"Sounds like a lot of trouble," Beckett says.

I look at him. "It's pretty easy to cook up some rice. Keep it in the fridge, offer it to him two or three times a day."

"Look, I'm not at home all that much. Why don't you just put him down?"

I freeze. "Are you serious?"

"Well, he's got this diarrhea ..."

"I'm sorry, Mr. Beckett, you'll have to find another vet."

His eyes widen, his brows shoot up. "Are you telling me you won't put him down?" His voice is incredulous.

"That's what I'm telling you. I won't put him down." We look at each other across the table, the dog between us. "Look,

Mr. Beckett, this is a young dog. He's got diarrhea, but no other symptoms, no problems that I can see. The diarrhea could be caused by a virus, some intestinal parasite, even something as simple as a dietary indiscretion."

"Dietary indiscretion?"

"Eating garbage or something spoiled. It could self-correct in a day or two."

"You mean he might get better on his own?"

"Yes. He might."

"You know," he says, leaning against the wall, "I pretty much abuse this dog."

Now I'm aghast. What on earth does he mean by that?

"I'm surprised you'd tell me that." My voice is ice. Gwynne is watching me, her mouth open, her eyes wide.

Beckett's eyes are unflinching in their gaze. As are mine.

"Go ahead and treat him," Beckett says, looking at the dog, running a hand down the dog's back. "And give him whatever vaccinations he needs. I'll pick him up later today. What time do you close?"

"Six o'clock," Gwynne says, shooting me a warning look. She takes Beckett by the arm and leads him out to the waiting room.

What did he mean, that he pretty much abuses the dog? Is this something I should report? I assume he meant he doesn't show the dog any attention, not that he actually harms the dog. I saw no injuries, no signs of mistreatment. The dog didn't cower, didn't act afraid.

He must have meant he doesn't give the dog much attention. Surely that's what he meant. Nonetheless, I'm furious.

A minute later it all drains away when I remember the puppy I put down this morning. Antifreeze poisoning. His dash to freedom the previous day cost him his life.

His breath had a sweet candy odor. He still looked so healthy, frisky, but his lab work told a different story. In another twelve hours he would have been suffering the worst kind of pain. Antifreeze poisoning is an awful way to die.

The owners wanted to take him home, hoping he'd get better on his own. The little girl looked at me, her dark eyes angry and defiant. "I don't want you to take my puppy," she said. She rubbed her eyes with a balled up fist. I heard the pleading in her voice. "My daddy gave him to me," she wailed.

If they'd brought him to me earlier, two to four hours after it happened, I might have been able to save him. But when I finally saw him, his kidneys were already compromised, ready to shut down.

"Look at that," Gwynne cries one morning. "The neuro kitty. She was looking out the window, feet up against the glass, and down she went. Her back legs just folded up." She picks up the kitten.

I take it from her and carry it back to the office I share with Dr. Sussman.

Sylvester, our beagle with the spinal cord injury, drags himself over to say hello. He sniffs the kitten, licks her face, then goes back to his blanket beneath my desk.

Gwynne approaches me that afternoon. She's heard of the plan to send the kittens to the research facility in Columbus.

"You can't do that," she tells me. "They're not your kittens. I'm the one who found them."

"They were surrendered to the practice, Gwynne."

"I'm gonna adopt them myself. Take them home with me. Both of them."

"Gwynne, you can't. You already have five cats. Their care would be so expensive, and they'd be alone all day. You just can't do it."

"You'd help me, wouldn't you? You'd treat them, give me samples? Take care of them?"

"It's not just a question of their care, Gwynne. You'd have to watch them get progressively worse. And honestly, they probably don't have long to live."

"That doesn't matter. At least I could give them a decent life, for whatever time they have left. If you give the kittens to this Dr. Reynolds, they'll spend the rest of their lives in cages. They'll never be able to go outside, never have normal lives. She'll experiment on them, implant things in their brains."

"She might be able to help them."

"She's a research doctor. She's interested in the disease, not in the kittens."

"She might want to observe them. Video them, document how the disease progresses. Footage like that would be invaluable in teaching about these diseases. At some point, she'll have to put them down, but that's exactly what will happen if you adopt them. If I take them to Columbus, we might be able to learn something about this condition. Dr. Reynolds might want to breed them ..."

"They're siblings," Gwynne cries out. "They're brother and sister."

"Well, she could breed them to other cats."

"No," Gwynne says. "They're mine. I found them. You can't have them."

They are not Gwynne's cats. I can do with them whatever I want. But it is a point I do not want to argue.

A week later she relents. "I'll let you have them," she says, "but only on the condition that you promise me any research that is done will benefit children."

"Children who have these diseases never become adults," I remind her.

It would be easy to promise, but I remember something I read in a research paper. In an attempt to learn how the diseases progress, a researcher set up a study involving six cats of the same age. Three had storage diseases, and three were normal. When the subjects were six weeks old, the researcher killed a storage cat and a normal cat in order to compare their brains. He killed another set at ten weeks, the third set at four months.

I can't make any promises to Gwynne.

"Surrender the kittens to her," Savannah messages me. "Dr. Reynolds was one of our smartest teachers. Think what it might mean for science. Think how much good might come of it."

"She might just euthanize them so she can study their brains," I message back.

"Research is important. Humans get these diseases."

"If I thought some good might come of it, if I knew for sure it would advance our knowledge of storage diseases, maybe lead to treatment or even a cure, I'd be thrilled. But what if it doesn't? What if I take these kittens to Columbus, and she isn't interested in studying them while they're alive? What if she designs some experiment like the one I read about on the internet?"

For this Savannah has no answer.

Andy weighs in. "It's a chance in a lifetime," he says. "Imagine what it could mean, to be able to contribute to a cause like this."

He knows I harbor a secret desire to go into research some day. I am intrigued by the mystery, the search for an answer, the hidden key, the puzzle, the logic.

"Where do you suppose that researcher I read about on the internet got three cats, all the same age, all with storage diseases?"

"He went to the shelter?"

"Not likely."

How did it happen, I wonder, that these two kittens ended up here, on my doorstep? That I saw the tremors, and I began to think of storage diseases? What should I do?

In the end, I let Gwynne have them. "Take them home," I tell her. "I'll provide what medical care I can."

It all goes against me with Sweetie. She's an orange tabby, 14 years old, the kind of cat that looks at you and starts to purr. A cat with a purr that sounds like an outboard motor. A cat who will purr when she's dying.

As this cat surely will, unless I can work some kind of miracle.

So often I wish I could practice without interference from the owners. Then someone like Connie Hinton comes along. She's about my age, 26 or so, a sixth-grade science teacher in a private school in Forest Hills. She's had Sweetie since she was a teenager. She's willing to spend any amount of money on the cat, learn medical techniques she can do at home, do whatever she has to do.

Connie is the perfect client. But then I find my skills aren't good enough. The medicine doesn't work the way it's supposed to work. Labs make mistakes. There are things I can't control. The cat suffers, and the owner suffers.

"She can no longer feel her feet," I tell Connie. "See how weak she is in her hind quarters?"

We're watching Sweetie try to walk across the table. Her back legs are bent, her gait peculiar, flat-footed. She moves forward in a kind of a half-crouch. "It's called the plantigrade stance. Neuropathy. Nerve damage from too much sugar in the blood."

Connie sighs. "Does it hurt? Is that why she's walking that way?"

"It probably hurts less when she walks that way."

Sweetie's problem is uncontrolled diabetes mellitus. The bladder infection she presented with has gone into her kidneys. Yesterday I sent a urine specimen to the lab and started her on antibiotics. Until I get the results of the culture, I have no way of knowing if I chose the right antibiotic.

"She was in perfect health when I moved in with my fiancé," Connie says. "Is it possible the dry food he keeps out for his cat could have caused this? When I lived by myself on Granberry, I always fed her Fancy Feast in the little cans."

"We don't know what causes diabetes. A high carbohydrate diet could be a contributing factor. There's some research to indicate that. Wet food is probably better for her. A good quality wet food. Or a high-protein dry food."

"I noticed it a few months after I moved. She was drinking water all the time, and using the litter box more than she ever did before. I saw she was losing weight. I could feel how skinny she was getting."

"What kind of dry food does he use?"

"He buys it at Walmart."

"They sell Iams."

"They sell Fancy Feast, too. It isn't Iams."

"There's another insulin I'd like to try. It's called Lantus. It's not as long lasting as the Humulins or the PZIs, but there are some studies indicating that if you combine this insulin with a carb-restricted diet, remission rates are actually quite high."

"You mean she could get over it? Not be diabetic anymore?"

"It's possible. Her blood sugar is out of control. Over 600. I think it's worth a shot."

She nods. "What we're using now surely isn't working. Six hundred. No wonder she has neuropathy."

"Let me have her for a few hours. I'll keep a close eye on her, I promise.

Come back later this afternoon."

Lantus is the most expensive of the insulins we prescribe, but the dosage is smaller, and the results are good. I've used it on two other cats. Both have gone into remission. Sweetie is older than either of them; I hope it works for her.

In the space of a half hour the injection brings Sweetie's blood sugar down to 140, then to 80. The sharp, downward trend is scary. When it drops to 50, I grab the Karo syrup and rub it on her gums. She doesn't like it, tries to get away from me. Her purring stops. But when I'm done, she instantly forgives me. She cleans her face and paws and begins to purr again.

Her blood sugar stabilizes at 80, and when Connie returns, I send Sweetie home with her. She knows her cat well enough that she can spot it if the blood sugar drops too low.

"Call me if she gets in trouble in the night," I tell Connie. "I'll be at home. Call me."

Four days later, there are still no lab results from the urine sample. Finally, on the fifth day, they tell me the specimen has been lost.

"You lost the urine sample I sent? You never did the culture?"

"It got pushed to the back of the refrigerator," the girl tells me. "By the time we found it, it was degraded to the point where we don't think the results would be reliable."

"My client paid $90 for that test, and you lost it? And you didn't bother to call me?"

"We'll be glad to do another culture for you, Dr. Wheeler. No charge, of course."

"What good will that do? I've already started antibiotics."

A week later, Sweetie is still hanging on. Connie brings her in nearly every day. The antibiotic appears to be working, but the Lantus is not. It's too effective, dropping her blood sugar too low. I switch her to Ultralenta, give Connie free samples, and when they're gone, a supply returned by a client who lost her cat.

The practice manager scrutinizes the statements before he gives them to Connie. He questions the techs about services rendered, drugs used. He thinks I'm spending too much time with this patient, giving away too much free care. I overhear Gwynne telling him about the lab test Connie paid for, but he is unimpressed.

"Labs make mistakes," he says.

At our last Thursday general meeting, the practice manager grudgingly read my stats. "Kylie bills out higher than anyone in the office," he said, "but she sees fewer patients."

He looked at me, and on his face I saw a blend of admiration and disdain. "She's carrying her own," he added.

I knew what he was thinking: that I order too many tests. I take too much time with my surgeries. The practice would make more money if I saw more patients.

But I am not a worker on an assembly line.

Sometimes I wish I were.

Connie is my perfect client, Sweetie the patient I want most to save.

But Sweetie rockets into renal failure, and it happens so swiftly there is nothing I can do.

The old man who can't read is back. His puppy is feverish, dehydrated, lethargic. I begin the examination while I'm running through the possibilities in my mind: parvovirus,

GI foreign body with possible perforation of the intestinal wall, a virus of some kind, fever of unknown origin.

"It's my fault," the old man says. "I tried to keep him away from the other dogs. I built a pen out behind my trailer, but he got out. Do you think you can help him? I'd like to take those papers you offered me the last time I was here. I'll find someone who can help me read them."

He watches while I take the dog's temp, look in his mouth, examine his feet, palpate his abdomen. X-rays rule out a foreign body in his intestinal tract. There's no vomiting or diarrhea, so it's probably not parvo. I give him fluids and prescribe antibiotics to cover a bacterial infection.

"Do you think I can work out a payment schedule?" the old man asks. "To take care of the bill?"

"Of course you can," I tell him. "Whatever you can afford will be okay." I hand him the booklet and instruction sheet. "I think your puppy's gonna be fine. Give it a few days and he'll be back to normal."

He looks skeptical.

"He's lucky to have you," I tell him.

He lowers his head, nods, and turns away.

I watch them leave the examining room. The puppy's head is resting on the old man's shoulder.

The kittens are nearly ten months old when Gwynne decides it's time. I've done what I could for them, but the disease has marched on, as we all knew it would.

Since the day Gwynne first took them home, I've been sending Dr. Reynolds regular reports on their condition.

She's tried to be helpful in suggesting treatment options. She says she completely understands why I could not bring them earlier.

We pick a day. Andy drives to Gwynne's apartment. Hope, the little female, can no longer walk. Gwynne carries her out to the car and lays her in my lap. Freddie, the male, is frightened. He has a wild look in his eyes, and he clings to Gwynne, his claws dug into her shoulder. I ask if he'd be better off in one of the carriers I've brought. Gwynne says no, that he doesn't like to be separated from his litter-mate.

She unhooks Freddie from around her neck and puts him in my lap next to Hope. He calms down almost immediately.

Their growth has been stunted by the disease, and they still seem like kittens to me. They sleep, curled around each other, as we cross the Mississippi River and head toward Columbus. The drive takes nearly seven hours.

When the outline of the city finally appears on the horizon, I feel relief tinged with regret. The time has come. In another hour, it will be done.

Andy parks by the admission entrance and turns off the engine. "We're here," he says.

"I'm glad Gwynne didn't come."

He reaches across to pet Freddie, who is awake and looking fearful. "You've done all you could for these little guys," he says.

"I have to do it, don't I? We've come all this way. I can't change my mind now." Freddie stretches and curls himself around his sister. They are warm in my lap, and I dread having to disturb them. "I almost wish I'd euthanized them," I add.

"Did you consider doing that?"

"Yes. More than once. If I could only be certain I'm doing the right thing, I wouldn't mind so much."

"You probably won't ever know that. But at least you know Dr. Reynolds. You know what kind of person she is."

"At least I know Dr. Reynolds." But is that a comfort? I don't really know what she's going to do with them. I can't put conditions on this surrender.

Andy gets out of the car, brings the larger carrier around to my side. We put both kittens inside and begin the long walk toward the main entrance of the building.

As I walk beside my husband down the path, I think about how it's always going to hurt. Whenever I have to do something like this, I'll feel the pain. It won't ever stop.

But maybe that's okay. What occurs to me is that if I ever stop hurting, if I ever get to the point where it's just a job, if I begin to think the lives of these creatures are worthless, their pain of no consequence, I'll give it up. I won't be a vet anymore. I'll look for some other line of work.

Acknowledgments

So many people have encouraged and supported me through the writing of this book.

My heartfelt thanks to Betty Blackburn, Phyllis Gobbell, Mary Buckner, Douglas Jones, John Bridges, Rick Romfh, Shannon Thurman, Corabel Shofner, Mary Bess Dunn, Martha Whitmore Hickman, Madeena Nolan, Chris Svitek, and others who listened, questioned, and critiqued.

To my first readers, I am especially indebted.

Finally, I am grateful beyond measure to my husband and my three daughters. He has always believed, as have they.

CPSIA information can be obtained
at www.ICGtesting.com
Printed in the USA
LVOW13s1955270517
536108LV00003B/29/P